Migrations in New Cinema

Cours de Poétique
London 2020

Migrations in New Cinema

Maeve Brennan
Sirah Foighel Brutmann and
   Eitan Efrat
Katrin Wahdat
Lana Askari
Sasha Litvintseva
Maha Maamoun
Edwina Attlee
Nicholas Brooks

Ektoras Arkomanis ed.

2 Endotic Investigations

Preface

'Every voyage is the unfolding of a poetic. The departure, the crossover, the fall, the wandering, the discovery, the return, the transformation. If traveling perpetuates a discontinuous state of being, it also satisfies, despite the existential difficulties it often entails, one's insatiable need for detours and displacements in postmodern thought.'

Trinh T. Minh-ha, *Elsewhere, within Here*[1]

This book was conceived in 2017, sometime between Richard Mosse's *Incoming* exhibition at the Barbican Centre and the theatrical release of Ai Wei Wei's *Human Flow*, two projects among so many in recent times that have used film to say something about the refugee experience. As I write this introduction, two years later, I am reading that millions of painted lady butterflies are arriving in the UK from Africa and Southern Europe – a mass migration that occurs roughly once every ten or eleven years – and I think back to Marc Silver's short film *There Are No Others, There Is Only Us*, which a decade ago used footage of half-a-million starlings manoeuvring in the sky to comment suggestively on human migration, borders, crowds and otherness.

'Migrations' here is a trope – a state of mind, a process or way of seeing, 'the unfolding of a poetic' through the contributing writers' own journeys or exiles, or as found in their subjects, whether in literal manifestations or by metaphorical readings.

The first part of the book is titled 'Returns' because it sees the authors returning to their homelands – all except Maeve Brennan, who revisits her great-grandfather's architectural work in Jerusalem a century ago. Her journey through time turns out differently than expected, by millions of years, as she scales socio-political layers against geological ones – expedient ons against slow occurrences related to stone in Palestine. eturning, in person or through writing, is a political act; it stems from consciousness of half-written or untold stories, and an urge to revisit singular accounts and correct them. Back in 1993 Edward Said perceived this kind of rectification as an antidote to cultural imperialism, and identified migrant thought as a vital ingredient:

> Yet it is no exaggeration to say that liberation as an intellectual mission … has now shifted from the settled, established and domesticated dynamics of culture to its unhoused, decentred, and exilic energies, energies whose incarnation today is the migrant, and whose consciousness is that of the intellectual and artist in exile, the political figure between domains, between forms, between homes, and between languages. From this perspective, then, all things are indeed counter, original, spare, strange.[2]

The shift in the winds in the early 1990s has played out in the films of the diaspora generation that followed. Lana Askari discusses what visual anthropology can reveal about Kurdish migration, and about social and individual imaginaries in Kobane. Her homecoming coincides with her subject-protagonist's exile, and their encounter is made possible by the recent liberation of Kobane from the Islamic State, so their exchanges feel grounded and transient at the same time. Katrin Wahdat lays out a triptych of stories about lives – actual and on film – branded by the phenomenon of *bacha posh* (bringing up girls as boys) in Afghanistan. These are imposed individual transformations in a society where primitive mores persist in the face of modernity. And yet, amid severity there are unexpected instances of freedom and tenderness.

Scale varies as collective and personal histories alternate.

Sasha Litvintseva considers how her exile from Rus
reconciled with sweeping political forces and narrat
ing from an 'elsewhere' in space or time allows one t
slower shifts which are only perceptible over longer periods of
time; in the case of my essay, the piecemeal changes of identity
that the area of Eleonas in Athens has undergone since the early
twentieth century through migrations, agriculture, industrialisation and decay.

The second part is titled 'Endotic Investigations' after Perec's
abstraction of an inverse anthropology that finds poetry in the
domestic and the quotidian (and by implication decolonises
the 'exotic'). The three pieces gathered here are painstaking
readings made between the lines; open-ended explorations
characterised by looking again, rewriting and rearranging until
the familiar is mystifying. In Maha Maamoun's film *Domestic
Tourism II* we see the Giza Pyramids again and again, in countless melodramatic, funny and banal scenes collected from films
made in Egypt from the 1950s to the present, and shown back to
back. The mental deconstruction of the famous monuments
continues into her 'scene typology' table presented in this book,
which inevitably brings about an unsettling sensation that the
monuments are dematerialising as their lore expands.

Edwina Attlee writes about Tom Phillips' project *20 Sites,
n Years*, which documents how London locations of no apparent
interest change over time, and Healy and Weber's *There They
Carved a Space*, a briefer but no less intense endeavour where
similar preoccupations with commonness mature into an atti-
tude. If monuments can no longer provide the fixed references
we seek amid urban incongruity, do we then replace them with
everyday objects and sites, or leftover forms found in a landscape, like Smithson did at Passaic in the 1960s? Watching the
geometric solids in Nicholas Brooks' film, you sense that they
stand in for something bigger. Have they been invited to replace

.ed icons? They seem to be types rather than personalities –
.iew kinds of monuments that like ancient masked actors let
you project character onto them. Their worth and significance
fluctuate as they turn up in different settings: in familiar paintings, in a car park installation or out in the countryside. The
mental distances of these transferences are almost unfathom-
able, and so the monumentality ascribed on these solids cannot
speak to us collectively, only individually.

Iconic monuments make appearances elsewhere too, but
not as embodiments of stability. We know that as a symbol the
Dome of the Rock is susceptible to ethno-religious conflict, but
Brennan's film shows it as physically vulnerable too. Depending
on the reading, the maintenance and perpetual transformation
of its tissue and structure can be reassuring or portentous, but
in any case we know where we are. More disorienting are the
depictions of monuments in Sirah Foighel Brutmann and Eitan
Efrat's film *Orientation*: the remains of the dome of the Shrine
of Salame, which are shown in a negative image, presumably to
mirror histories of erosion and erasure; and the White Square
monument, first glimpsed through a frenzied camera looking
down at the pavement, then through a series of overexposed
images of the square, as if a white haze has arrived from the sea
and settled on this outpost of Tel Aviv. When we're finally up on
the monument and looking out through the muddy glass, the
uncertainty is somewhat alleviated by views of the surroundings, and by the architect's storytelling, transposed from an
email onto the screen.

Equally hard to assuage is the historical disorientation that
the replica of the Cathedral of Christ the Saviour in Moscow
triggers in Litvintseva, who rightly views it as a farcical and
tragic forgery of collective identity. How can filmmakers account
for such disruptions and ambiguities? Creating a film out of
entirely unoriginal material, making screen postcards, digging

out photos from family albums, taking up 'erasing' text in old novels, projecting films onto one's body, or loading some archetypal forms onto the top of a car and taking them out for a drive – these are some of the methods deployed by the films in question. Meanwhile, the filmmaker's mind undergoes successive transformations; it morphs into a migrant nous adopting a multitude of perspectives over a single film or sequence: the exile's, the historian's, the journalist's, the anthropologist's, the archaeologist's, the tourist's, Google Street View and other.

So are we verging towards clarity or receding into arcane representations? I think that throughout the book there is a calm acceptance that entanglement precedes elucidation and is therefore a necessary stage, whatever comes next; that official versions of events will not do even if one is not entirely comfortable with postmodern fragmentation; and that diversity of methods and perspectives does not preclude commitment to the big questions and themes of modernity.

It makes sense to begin at Jerusalem, a perennial locus of conscience and conflict, and to end up at a remote somewhere, nowhere in particular. It could have worked the other way round too, but it seems right to proceed from the historically charged to an open landscape, where we can let the stories of the book revisit us in whatever order or form they might.

Ektoras Arkomanis (London, autumn 2019)

1   Trinh T. Minh-ha, *Elsewhere, within Here*
     (London: Routledge, 2010), 40.
2   Edward Said, *Culture and Imperialism*
     (London: Chatto and Windus, 1993), 403.

1 Returns

Jerusalem Pink

Maeve Brennan

Jerusalem gold polished (high density), Jerusalem gold rough block, Jerusalem bone cream, Benjamin grey (hard), Deep blue (honed), Hebron gold, Hebron yellow, Hebron bone, Bone light (polished), Halila beige, Hebron white red veins, Hebron pink (brushed), Jerusalem royal, Ramon white, Birzeit gold, Jerusalem shells, Jerusalem rose, Jerusalem golden veins, Palestinian grey (honed), Palestinian cream (hard), Desert yellow, Negev fossil, Hebron snow, Jerusalem ivory, Jerusalem pink.

> During more than twelve hundred years
> the building has been exposed to the destructive attacks of
> winter storms
> of summer suns
> of earthquakes
> of fire
> and of 'souvenir' seekers
>
> The weather does not attack all sides of the octagon with
> the same severity
>
> Repairs have been made at distinct intervals
> Change has been a condition of the building's existence
> had there been no change
> the building would have disappeared[1]

Maeve Brennan, *Jerusalem Pink* (UK, 2015). A Jerusalem stone quarry in use at night. The quarry is located beside Qalandiya checkpoint, the main entry point between Jerusalem and the northern West Bank.

Travelling in the West Bank, I have the surreal but disturbingly common experience of driving alongside a mountain only to find that it abruptly stops halfway in a sharp vertical line, its interior made visible, containing traces of the industrial processes used to extract its stone. The architecture of the landscape is rapidly shifting due to the unregulated growth of the stone industry, now the backbone of the Palestinian economy. Inverse spaces appear where mountainous terrain would have once stood. Quarries are an architecture of by-product, born out of a process of extraction, physical evidence of the disappearance of the West Bank.

Much of the extracted stone contributes to the construction and expansion of Israel – stone cladding, settlements, suburbs. Faced with a convoy of lorries, each one filled to the top with construction materials, a sense of severe unease comes over me, a sort of anxiety bound to construction. I am aware of the constant expansion and development of 'facts on the ground' – that these raw materials will soon conflate to form a settlement or outpost. I came to Palestine with the intention of researching my great-grandfather's role as architect during the British Mandate but was quickly waylaid by more current events.

I am in a 4×4 with Abdelhamid, driving to his limestone quarry in the mountains close to Nablus. On the ascent to Juma'een, I see what looks like a volcano erupting dust, with white plumes of smoke enveloping the surrounding village. On my right, there is a large pool of opaque white liquid coated with a pearlescent sheen. It seems that the limestone from the quarry is seeping into the local environment in whatever form. In fact, there are seventeen Jerusalem stone excavation sites surrounding this tiny village. A short walk through it leaves our clothes covered in a thin layer of white dust.

Abdelhamid's quarry cuts deep into the mountainside, exposing limestone walls 100 ft high. The layers of strata are rough and beige at the top, smooth and pink further down. In a region so dense with historical significance, the sight of strata resonates. I think of Eyal Weizman's politics of verticality – the divvying up of contested sites into layers, like the Israeli archaeological digs spreading out beneath the Dome of the Rock, which are putting its foundations at risk.[2]

***

The Persian artists first clothed the Dome of the Rock
The tiles have been replaced in some form or other
We see today a complex result of the efforts made
by perhaps as many as fifteen generations of men

Ernest Richmond was invited to Palestine in 1917 by the British Mandate government. His role was to survey the condition of the Dome of the Rock. He spent six months in a drawing studio,

Fig. 55 bis. East face of Octagon. Northern half

First Period   Second Period   Third Period   Fourth Period   Fifth Period   Sixth Period

'Fig. 55 bis. East face of Octagon. Northern half', from *The Dome of the Rock in Jerusalem: A Description of its Structure and Decoration* (Oxford: Clarendon Press, 1924). A diagram, by Ernest Richmond, of the eastern face of the Dome of the Rock, depicting the six instances of tile restorations that were carried out on the exterior of the Dome of the Rock across fourteen centuries.

inside a small domed building in a corner of the Haram al Sharif, carrying out a forensic investigation of the building. He eventually published his findings in 1924 in a volume titled *The Dome of the Rock: A Description of Its Structure and Decoration*. At the back of the book there are sixteen drawings based on sixteen photographs. Each drawing depicts half a facet of the octagonal structure, with shading of various densities and patterns that denote time periods (First Period, Second Period, Third Period ...). The six time periods correspond to the six instances of major restoration carried out on the tile work that clothes the exterior of the building. These restorations took place across fourteen centuries.

The diagrams can at first appear abstract. The irregularly shaped shifts in surface disguise the architectural forms present (arches, windows, cornices). These forms are a reminder of the physical building that the drawings describe. We might read these drawings as diagrams of time. The constant maintenance and repair necessary for the building to endure is made visible in a patchwork of historical eras, the walls themselves rendered as historical documents.

Richmond writes in the introduction to his survey: 'The Dome of the Rock is, then, alive – almost in the same sense that a man is alive. It changes its tissues and it renews its structure in order to maintain power to enshrine the soul that is in it.'[3]

***

Some columns are encircled with iron bands
necessitated by the marble having split
no doubt caused by earth tremors
Metal ties are of no use in a serious movement
but they act as a safeguard when slight tremors occur

The columns are of coloured marbles with gilded capitals
Both columns and capitals belonged to former buildings

Jerusalem stone comes from indigenous Cretaceous and Tertiary rocks that belong to the Turonian period and consist of Limestone, Dolomite and sometimes chalk. The texture on the stone's surface that gives it its particular character is

NO DOUBT CAUSED BY EARTH TREMORS

Maeve Brennan, *Jerusalem Pink* (UK, 2015). A block of Jerusalem stone sliced by a stone-cutting machine.

owed to an abundance of marine carbonate sediments.[4] It takes approximately 90 million years to form.

In 1918, during the British Mandate, Colonel Ronald Storrs (one of Richmond's colleagues) ordered that only local limestone should be used in the construction of buildings, extensions and rooftops in the Old City of Jerusalem. This stone bylaw was then more strictly imposed by Israel as part of the 1968 Master Plan, an urban development scheme for the 'unification' of the areas within the newly expanded boundaries of Jerusalem.[5] Every structure within these boundaries was to be clad in Jerusalem stone. The aim was to produce a visual coherence across these disparate areas, 'helping them appear as organic parts of the city' that carry 'emotional messages that stimulate other sensations embedded in collective memory, producing ... strong associations to the ancient holy city of Jerusalem.'[6] Socio-political forces, national identity and collective memory are all forged into the material fabric of Jerusalem stone.

Maeve Brennan   19

The cladding conceals structures built predominantly from brick, concrete and cinderblocks. Over the past five decades, these façades have thinned and current building regulations permit just 60mm-thick sawn stone. The stone's ancientness is intended to provide a visual legitimacy to the expanded suburbs of Jerusalem by introducing a consistent historical texture.

**

They say embroidered cloths hung like a tent
over the sacred rock
held in place by thick ropes of silk

Upon finding a small mineral collection, mounted on aged white cartridge paper and inside a thin plywood frame, I decide to call the number printed on the bottom right, underneath an example of glittery white quartz from Nazareth. The collection is titled *MINERALS, ROCKS & FOSSILS FROM THE HOLY LAND: Treasures from Around the Greatest Rift in the World, Collections of Dr. Taleb Al-Harithi, Ph.D. Geology.* Dr. Taleb answers and we swiftly arrange to meet in Hebron the following Wednesday. I ask that he kindly send me his email address in case I need further details. Moments later, I receive a text message reading only 'GEOLOGYTALEB@GMAIL.COM.' We meet at a shawarma place that looks out over the corner of a busy main road in Hebron, and he proceeds to explain emphatically, 'If you blindfold me and take me in an airplane to anywhere in Palestine, wherever you drop me I would be able to tell where I am from the rocks.'

**

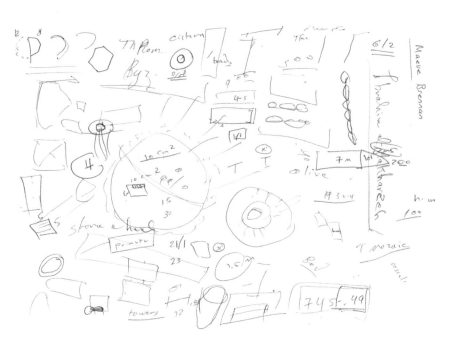

Sketch of archaeological sites in the southern West Bank, drawn by archaeologist Dr Ibrahim Mekharzeh during our first meeting (West Bank, January 2015).

The paving rests upon a bed composed of earth and lime
saturated with moisture
Plants have established their roots in thick masses under
the stones

I meet Dr Ibrahim at a municipal building in a village south of Hebron. I had been told he can show me a number of archaeological sites, relating to the history of the stone industry in Palestine. He sits down and says 'Maeve, I was born in a cave.' He takes a pen and paper and writes his name clearly at the top, passing me the pen so I can write mine. He begins to describe the various relevant sites, drawing as he speaks, depicting each significant stone with a small rectangle and each olive press with a circle. Over the course of the meeting he fills the A4 page with shapes, measurements and the odd word or half-word:

stone wheel
Byz
cistern
vessels
T mozaic [sic]
towers
beads
olive
Throne
Bed

Dr Ibrahim Mekharzeh is a well-known Palestinian archaeologist who has worked on many important excavations in the south. On our tour of the sites we are obliged to stop for five

Maeve Brennan, *Jerusalem Pink* (UK, 2015). Dr Ibrahim Mekharzeh gesturing at significant archaeological sites in the distance (southern West Bank).

Jerusalem Pink

visits with friends he has made during his time working in the area. A man with nine children – and two wives, the doctor quietly warns me – sits us in his garden and serves us coffee. It is time for prayer, and Dr Ibrahim brings out a jug of water to wash his hands. He carefully chooses a wild flower to kneel beside, making sure the excess water falls upon it.

Later we arrive at a Byzantine quarry. Dr Ibrahim gestures at the hilltop and narrates how ancient industry inscribed itself on the landscape. I begin to see remnants of carved stone steps where blocks of stone have been chiselled out in layers. He tells me that water was sometimes used in the extraction process, poured into cracks where it would freeze and expand, dislodging blocks of stone. He strokes the manmade marks still present on the limestone surface with his finger.

***

There was a tradition among the guardians of the building
that when the remains of the mosaic were removed
to allow the walls to be prepared for the tiles
the mosaics were buried in various places in the Haram area
Some under raised platforms
others under flights of steps

A quantity of fragments were found
It would be worthwhile to attempt their reassemblage and
decipherment

I arrive in Jerusalem with the hope of getting inside the Dome of the Rock to film. I have been in touch with Beatrice St Laurent, a Canadian academic whose name came up when I entered 'politics of the restoration of the Dome of the Rock' into Google. She tells me she will be staying at the Albright Institute for Archaeological Research in East Jerusalem in January, and to come for tea. She has been searching for a relative of Ernest Richmond, who remains something of a gap in her research.

During my visit, we discuss her work on Peter McGaw, Richmond's successor at the Haram al Sharif. Her research has been greatly aided by Isam Awwad, resident architect at the Dome of the Rock for the past thirty-two years but recently retired. He arrives during my visit and offers to assist me with getting access to the site. I am to draft a letter to the Awqaf stating clearly that I am the great-granddaughter of Ernest Tatham Richmond, and he will pass it on. A week later I receive their approval.

I am permitted to enter between dawn and midday prayer. The shrine is relatively empty at this time, except for the care-taker, who is vacuuming the vast octagonal carpet. The intricately patterned marble walls match the exterior. I think of something cousin Susanna recalled Ernest saying – 'Upon taking down the tiles of the Dome of the Rock, it was found that the underside was as carefully worked as the front.'

The central atrium that encloses the rock is boarded up like a building site, with a lattice of scaffolding climbing up toward the 20-metre high dome. Isam leaves me with one of the conservators, who eventually asks if I would like to accompany him to the top. We ascend the scaffold, closely passing marble decorations, elaborate stained glass and shimmering gold leaf, usually only visible at a considerable distance. Prayer mats are slung over horizontal scaffold poles at various heights. We reach the top and come out onto a circumference of wooden plank flooring where eight men are at work on the green, red and golden relief that fills the giant dome. Isam told me that due to an unsuccessful restoration by the Egyptians, water had entered through the roof and damaged the ornate interior.

Standing inside it, the scale of the dome is stunning. The restorers working on the other side appear tiny but the sounds

Maeve Brennan, *Jerusalem Pink* (UK, 2015). Restorers at work on the dome's interior decorations inside the Dome of the Rock.

of their work echo round, and I hear the scratches of sandpaper as if they were right behind me. One of the men is singing as he's working, and his voice travels too. We approach the restorers, walking past a small seating area with plastic chairs, patterned cushions and a kettle for coffee. Two of the older men are working alongside two younger men, carefully observing their work and guiding them through the process. The older man puts on white latex gloves and begins to cut brown hessian into small pieces. The younger man dips them in PVA before inserting them into cracks in the relief. Up close the ornate detailing appears strangely large, and the damage is suddenly visible. Peeling green and red paint, cracked gold leaf, damp stains and gaps in the wooden structure forced open by years of rain and snow. One restorer is injecting glue into the loose surface with a syringe. I speak with the oldest conservator, who tells me he has worked at the Dome of the Rock for the past forty years, carrying out the constant restoration necessary for the building's health. He says only one other woman has been up to the Dome in that time – Beatrice St Laurent, during the restoration of the 1990s. And that of course my great-grand-father would have stood where I am standing now.

Notes

1   Indented paragraphs are quotes from Ernest Richmond, *The Dome of the Rock in Jerusalem: A Description of Its Structure and Decoration* (Oxford: Clarendon Press, 1924). Some of the original text and layout has been adapted.
2   Eyal Weizman, *Hollow Land: Israel's Architecture of Occupation* (London: Verso, 2007).
3   Richmond, *The Dome of the Rock*, 4.
4   Weizman, *Hollow Land*, 274.
5   This included the Old City, 28 Palestinian villages, the western Israeli city and the previously Jordanian-administered city.
6   The 1968 Master Plan, in Weizman, *Hollow Land*, 28.

References

Richmond, Ernest. *The Dome of the Rock in Jerusalem: A Description of Its Structure and Decoration*. Oxford: Clarendon Press, 1924.
Weizman, Eyal. *Hollow Land: Israel's Architecture of Occupation*. London: Verso, 2007.

Orientation

Sirah Foighel Brutmann
and Eitan Efrat

When I arrived here, to this house

that my father built some seventy years ago

even seventy-nine years ago,

I was four years old

and there was nothing here

There were a few small square houses

that an architect had built according to the International Style

very simply structures

and here and there new buildings were starting to appear

So there is no doubt that I was influenced by this place

So there is no doubt that I was influenced by this place

but I was not consciously thinking of it

The square was conceived as something completely formal

as a shape that corresponds with another shape

Only later did I decide to dedicate it
to the Founders of Tel Aviv

That's when the pyramid came to represent a tent

which relates to the tent my parents lived in on the beach

which relates to the tent my parents lived in on the beach

when they first arrived to Tel Aviv

I decided to construct it with white concrete

I had a specialist from Paris
who came to supervise the work

There were those who told me:
'why white concrete? it'll be black tomorrow!'
It is white and we never painted it

I thought that even if we were to paint it one day

and someone would scratch the paint

It'd still be white underneath and not grey

Then I planned to build a dome structure

and thought of planting weeds on it

so that the weeds would grow out of the dome like hair

similar to old dome structures that we have here

But instead I decided to plant an olive tree inside the dome

for the olive tree to grow with time.
It almost covers the dome by now

And why an olive tree?
Not only for what it symbolises

but because there are no olive trees in this park

I didn't use a tree I found in the park,
but one that I brought from somewhere else

I invited an organ specialist to constructs a pipe-flute

and together with an Israeli composer,
we composed a specific chord

which produces sound with the wind coming from the west

I wanted it to resemble the sound of the ships

like the sound of the ships' whistles that we used to hear when they arrived

to the port of Jaffa and the port of Tel Aviv

I wanted it to be a reminder of that sound

When you stand on the surface of the White Square the sea is hidden behind the city

when you stand at the top of the staircase you clearly see a thin blue line

Orientation

The Shrine of Salame stood at the centre of the ancient Palestinian village of the same name. The remains of its dome structure can still be seen in what is today the Kfar Shalem neighbourhood of Tel Aviv. The Palestinian village, which dates back to the sixteenth century, was until 1948 located on the highway connecting Jaffa Port to the mainland. During the Nakba of 1948 it was occupied by the Israeli army on behalf of the new Zionist state, and was then immediately evacuated. Within weeks of the expulsion of the Palestinian villagers from their land, the Israeli authorities that were in charge of the Jewish immigration repopulated the village with Yemenite Jews, who settled in the existing Palestinian stone houses. Today, while the ownership of the land is still in dispute, the Jewish and other Israeli residents of Kfar Shalem are threatened with evacuation by a construction company's plan to demolish the original houses and replace them with profitable flats and shops.

In 1989 the Israeli sculptor Dani Karavan completed White Square, a monument commissioned by the Municipality of Tel Aviv for an eastern outskirt of the city. Karavan decided to dedicate the sculpture to the founders of Tel Aviv, among whom was his father Abraham Karavan, the city's official landscape architect for four decades, beginning in the 1930s. The sculpture is composed of simple geometrical forms made out of white concrete – an influence from the International Style which was prominent in the early architecture of Tel Aviv. White Square is situated at the highest point of the area and only a few hundred metres south of the Shrine of Salame. In Arabic the commonly used name for the hill is Batikh Hill (Watermelon Hill).

Sirah Foighel Brutmann and Eitan Efrat

Bachagona Posh: Girls Growing Up as Boys in Afghanistan

Katrin Wahdat

'If you pass under a rainbow, a boy turns into a girl,
and a girl turns into a boy.' Afghan myth[1]

'Me and my sisters were running endlessly to try and catch the rainbow. We wanted to turn into a boy.'[2] My mother remembers a moment from her childhood. We all know passing under a rainbow is impossible – same as a girl turning into a boy, she tells me – but sadly, this is the dream of so many young girls in Afghanistan. Adults nurture this dream, which is planted into their innocent brains from an early age and doesn't fade as they grow old. The obsession with the male child and the preference for boys exist as consequences of patriarchal society, and are reinforced by religion and the longstanding traditions of Afghanistan.[3] When my mother was growing up, on national holidays like Eid, Norooz[4] and on other festive days, boys were allowed out on the streets, in community centres and other public spaces. They would climb walls and jump roofs while flying their kites, dive into the river with or without clothes, ride their bikes from street to street and play football on vast greens. Boys were allowed to participate in school trips, and in music and dance performances. When they were old enough they could even drive their fathers' cars to neighbouring towns.[5]

What did girls do in the meantime? They helped their mothers – as they still do – with every household duty: washing clothes, cleaning, ironing, cooking and taking care of their younger siblings. Their lives and actions were controlled by their parents while they secretly wished to go out and play with their friends.

In Afghanistan being a boy is every girl's dream because childhood for a boy brings the promise of freedom and fun.[6] Parents prefer to have sons; the more sons, the better their reputation, and the higher the esteem they are held in. Afghan society places a high value on sons because they can provide for the family and pass on its name to their descendants. Sons stay in the family; daughters leave when they get married.[7] The pride in having a son continues to the present day, having arguably gained traction with the passage of time.[8] This has always been a problem for families that have more daughters or only daughters, and at some indeterminable point the preference for boys manifested in the tradition of *buchagona posh*. Bachagona posh refers to a girl being disguised as a boy and presented as the family's son.[9]

My essay is an exploration of the bachagona posh phenomenon as a locus of complex histories of gender relations and deeply rooted traditions in Afghanistan. I examine three cases of bachagona posh: Habiba, my mother's school friend, who was a bachagona posh in the 1970s; the main character in the 2003 film *Osama*, set in Afghanistan at the time of the Taliban regime; and my grandmother, who appears as a boy in a family photograph from the late 1930s.

My grandmother, aged five and dressed in boys' clothes, posing for a photograph between her uncles. Proud – with raised chin and folded arms – and trying to look like an adult.

An invisible daughter

In Afghanistan, parents who have a son can look forward to less worry than those who have a daughter because a daughter is exposed to the scrutiny of society; she is constantly observed and judged. What a girl wears and how she behaves in public reflect on her mother, father and older brothers. The girl herself lives in constant anxiety or fear because the way she behaves, the loudness of her laugh and, of course, her physical appearance are all criteria on which others judge her family. For parents, allowing a daughter out in public inevitably translates into putting the family's reputation at risk.[10]

Bachagona posh is a tactic that can help a family overcome the perceived shortcoming of having a daughter, while also shielding the girl from society's watchful eye. Bachagona posh makes a daughter temporarily 'invisible.'[11] An extreme example of an invisible daughter is depicted in the film *Osama*. A girl, living in Kabul under the Taliban regime, is turned into a boy. Even though bachagona posh was at that time a common practice, the Taliban explicitly forbade women from dressing as men as part of their enforcement of gender segregation by every means available. Women lost all their rights; they were not allowed to work or to be seen on the street without a male escort, who had to be a close relative.[12] Having lost all its male members to the war, the protagonist's family struggles to even get food. In order to survive, the girl's grandmother and mother decide to make her into a bachagona posh and send her to work under the male name Osama.[13] In a society that denies women recognition and fundamental rights, bachagona posh emerges as a solution.

Perhaps surprisingly, the desire for sons does not necessarily originate with the father of the family. It is often the mothers that wish for a son, so they can acquire the reputation and high status that Afghan society bestows on mothers of male children.

The Golden Age of Afghanistan, from 1930–70, brought many positive changes on gender-related issues, but people were not prepared to completely break with established traditions.[14] This is evident in my case study of Habiba, who was born into a modern Afghanistan in the 1970s. Habiba was made a bachagona posh by her mother, who had failed to conceive a son. She took the decision fearing that her husband would leave her unless she gave birth to a son. There was also a super-stition that if a mother looks at a male child every day, her next child will be a son, so maybe in this case bachagona posh was employed in desperation, as a tool for conceiving a real son.[15] Despite her efforts, Habiba's father still went on to marry another woman, to try again for a son.

A free child

Colin Ward suggests that for most people the best childhood memory is of a moment when they felt like they were not a child.[16] Habiba's best memory of her childhood was from when she wore her dad's *karakul* hat – a traditional hat made of lambswool – and showed it off to the boys with whom she played on the streets. The boys did not know she was a girl. She never made a mistake, so they never found out. In contrast to other girls, Habiba did not feel intimidated around boys. She did not care whether she played with boys or girls; she felt comfortable among either. In a conversation over the phone Habiba reaffirms that she had thoroughly enjoyed her role of a bachagona posh.[17] It had afforded her significantly more freedom and possibilities than the other girls.

Habiba was the only bachagona posh at my mother's school, Lycée Zarina, a girls' school in Baghlan, Afghanistan. Her boyishness was expressed through her short hair and her clothes – she was the only pupil who wore trousers. Her demeanour was rascally and aggressive, especially in physical education class, where she felt she had to behave like a boy. She was a 'naughty spirit,' enjoying everything that the boys did, like jumping into swimming pools or onto the back of lorries. Her favourite activities became smoking cigarettes and setting things on fire with matchsticks.[18] The stereotypical activities of girls and boys were vastly different, but she was able to explore and enjoy either world as she chose. For example, she recalls that after school, while her sister would stay at home to study with their father; she would instead join the after-school lessons organised exclusively for boys because they were more exciting. But when the boys had to go to the mosque for Quran lessons, she often decided not to go.[19] There were also times when being a disguised girl got her into trouble:

> I will never forget when my dad took me to the tailor to make
> a suit for me. In the end we couldn't afford a suit and I only
> got a jacket. At first he wanted me to have trousers and a jacket.
> So the tailor took measurements of my leg and asked: 'Little
> boy, does your penis lean to the left or to the right?' I was so
> ashamed and shocked when he said those words.[20]

A collective secret

Habiba confirms that a lot of people outside of school didn't know she was a girl. Even though bachagona posh is not uncommon, most families keep it a secret. Indeed, it is a collective secret in Afghan society, a known lie that no one confronts, and which is inevitably challenged when the child reaches puberty and the feminine features become harder to disguise. Therefore, the transition back into a girl usually takes place before puberty, and it is not risk-free for the girl or for her family's reputation, as her chances of getting married might be compromised.[21]

Habiba wanted to keep her male identity. She resisted long hair, wearing dresses and skirts, earrings and jewellery, and instead wore the *peran tumban*, a traditional tunic for males, which helped her cover up her breasts. Habiba blames her parents for giving her this role because the feeling of being male has since been manifest in her personality – she never underwent a complete transition back to a female.

The closest she came was when she substituted women's trousers for men's. She remembers the first time she wore women's trousers; she kept tugging at them because she wasn't used to the high rise. Meanwhile, the male trousers she wore during her childhood sat so tightly around the hip that the development of her uterus was affected. Later in life, when Habiba struggled to get pregnant, the doctors diagnosed her with an underdeveloped uterus. She only conceived one son during her marriage, which did not last long.

Habiba now lives as a divorced single woman in Canberra, Australia. She believes that her bachagona posh period influenced her gender identity physically and mentally. She has a complex sexuality that confuses her; she does not see herself as a woman or a man.[22] She imagines that if she had been in Australia during her early twenties she might have been lesbian or bisexual. In Kabul she'd had a big crush on someone before she got married. She even had a boyfriend, which is very uncommon in Afghan culture, but as soon as the relationship became a little more serious she stepped back. She explains that in her childhood she was equal to boys and could now never accept a male's attempt to dominate her.[23]

In the Western World, a child has the right to an identity.[24] In Afghanistan if parents decide to change a child's gender, society plays along. There are no children's rights to protect them from their parents' will. Even schools support the parents in keeping up the practice of bachagona posh. Daughters have no power against this; they are obliged to wear what the mother provides for them.[25]

Sarah Ahmed understands willfulness as a character trait that is designated by other people but that can also be cultivated as a reaction to this designation. If we go by Ahmed's theory, bachagona posh has a more complex, potentially dangerous implication for the child. One way of looking at this is that the clothes of a bachagona posh constitute the adults' designation of the child's willfulness, while the girl's body is the willfulness archive of the girl herself.[26] When these two iterations of willfulness are in conflict, this becomes a precarious situation.

In the case of *Osama*, the mother's will for her family's survival propels her to dress her daughter in a peran tumban and send her out to work. This is in conflict with the girl's will, which manifests itself through her tears in the scene of her transition, as well as her expressions throughout the film. The peran tumban becomes the willfulness archive of the mother and the tears reveal the willfulness of the child. And yet, lines can be blurred when the bachagona posh has a strong self-will, like Habiba: in this case the state of bachagona posh can become part of the willfulness of the child, an instrument at the child's disposal, with which to provoke the controlling adults.[27]

An artefact of fashion

A common belief in Afghanistan is that 'what sets little boys and girls apart is all exterior: pants versus skirts. That, and the knowledge that those with pants always come first.'[28] During Afghanistan's Golden Age, for example, bachagona posh meant changing from skirts to pants.[29] But fashion and mores change with the times, and bachagona posh does not remain unaffected by these changes. The prevalence of the Taliban in 1996 caused a drastic change in the life of Afghans. Women had to wear burkas and cover every part of the body, and men had to wear the peran tumban and grow a full beard.[30] Besides the changes in clothing, women lost all rights, were denied education and had no freedom.

This is why Osama's transformation into a boy was more radical than Habiba's. It was a drastic change in all aspects of her life. Before her transition she was covered with a *chādor* and hardly showed any skin.[31] As a bachagona posh, suddenly Osama had to expose her face to men and, to be convincing as a boy, she had to change her behaviour in an instant; to look down and never directly into other people's eyes, for example, or to move and speak subtly, almost unnoticeably, which is, ironically, what women had to do at the time. During the Taliban regime gender segregation became so strict that girls and women were kept amongst themselves, and boys and men within groups that were exclusively male. Young girls hardly ever had contact with males. Osama's situation was even more extreme because she did not have any male relatives. For Osama bachagona posh was a double shock because the political insensitivity towards gender displaced her into the unfamiliar environment of men.[32] Bachagona posh in this case was imposed as an act of survival, and the child was doomed in that role.[33]

Through her research Jenny Nordberg discovered that

bachagona posh from poor families were forced into child labour and had to do things against their will, whereas the bachagona posh in better-off families enjoyed freedom and had fun in their role.[34] Being a boy from a poor family entailed child labour and portended an unpleasant childhood. Nordberg believes that regardless of the wealth and circumstances of the family, the motive behind turning a girl into a bachagona posh is always traced back to the family being in need of a son, and that this need is created by society.[35] But the nature of the need varies according to wealth and social status.

A doll

In contrast to Nordberg's findings, the case of my grandmother, is one that cannot be fully explained by financial circumstances or social recognition. Her family was rich and enjoyed a high status, and her parents did not care about the sex of their first-born. This is often the case in well-educated, liberal Afghan families that can afford to send their children to school and higher education.

My grandmother does not remember much from her bachagona posh childhood; she was still very young when she transitioned back into a daughter. When I ask her about a photograph that was taken when she was around five years old, she recalls that she felt proud to look like a boy, wearing three-quarter-length trousers and standing between her two uncles. That her uncles were holding hands attests that this was a moment of pride. I ask if she enjoyed that moment. 'Of course,' she answers. 'Every child would have been happy to be allowed to stand for a photograph.' I ask her what the girls of the family did instead. 'There were no girls in the family. Later, when my sisters were born, there were girls in the family.'

My grandmother, aged five, sat on the lap of her father who shows affection by holding his daughters cheeks between his hands.

It seems that my grandmother was not made a bachagona posh so that her family's position would improve. She tells me that her father would have loved her the same whether she had been born a boy or a girl. Another picture shows her in the arms of her father, whose affection is obvious – he is holding her cheeks as if intending to give her a kiss. Her aunts from her father's side had wished her to be a bachagona posh because she was their brother's first-born and they had *schauk* to have a nephew. Schauk is an Afghan expression that does not have a satisfactory translation into English; a combination of 'passion' and 'amusement' comes close. Her parents prioritised entertaining the aunts' will over allowing their daughter's willfulness to manifest itself.

Bachagona posh does appear not to have had any adverse effect on my grandmother's life, as she transitioned back to being a girl at the age of seven, before any of her brothers were born. She remembers the day; the whole family went for a picnic and celebrated her transition. But when I ask her if she remembers whether she was happy to be turned back into a girl, she replies, laughing: 'I am not sure. Now, I wish I had stayed a boy.'[36] Following the conversation with my grand-mother, I speak to my grandfather, who surprises me with some hitherto unknown and unexpected information: 'Sometimes, in Afghanistan, when a family did not have a son, they dressed one of their daughters as a boy. The other way round, when a family did not have a daughter, they dressed one of their sons as a girl.'[37]

It appears that adults found amusement in dressing their children in clothes of their choice, almost like playing with dolls. Children became a game for the adults of the upper class. The ultimate effect on the child's life was not considered in either case. The assertion that sons were also being turned into daughters does not rebut any of the prior findings about the motives and circumstances of those who were made into bachagona posh; instead it seems to reinforce the fact that adults control the life and identity of the child, no matter what the direction of the experiment.

I have found no evidence of the existence of *dokhtargona posh* (boys dressed as girls) but I find myself believing the words of my grandfather. In Afghanistan we tend to rely on information passed down by the elders, as record keeping has always been poor, and when it's not the record is often based on the knowledge and hearsay of men anyway.[38] In a country of many tribes, and with a high illiteracy rate, poetry and stories are more consequential than documents because everyone can memorise them in their native language – *dari* or *pashto* – and most knowledge is based on and perpetuated by oral history.[39]

Similarly, besides Nordberg's recent book *The Underground Girls of Kabul*, this essay relies on the collection of memories of people I have spoken to, and on the story told in the film *Osama*. There is often no other type of record. The United Nations and several other governmental and non-governmental organisations have refused to acknowledge the existence of bachagona posh.[40] Therefore, it was important for me to tell these very personal and previously untold stories, so that the suppressed case of bachagona posh children in Afghanistan is brought to light.

Conclusion

The bachagona posh phenomenon stems from a lack of gender equality in Afghan society, and has persisted in the absence of children's rights. Children in Afghanistan are regarded as the property of their parents and, as such, their will is oppressed. The oddity of girls dressed as boys seems paradoxical for one of the strictest countries regarding gender segregation. But in Afghanistan truth matters little and rules can be bent where gain of any kind is involved.[41] From a Western point of view, the existence of bachagona posh is not traceable because exclusivity undermines established truths. Tradition has proved time and again far more powerful than government, and has created a barrier of comprehension for outsiders.[42]

Afghanistan has been damaged by yet another seemingly endless conflict. As a result, children's and women's rights continue to be undermined. If one understands the spirit of a poetic and storytelling culture, the phenomenon of bachagona posh becomes instantly more plausible. Bachagona posh are regarded as real sons in Afghan culture because society chooses fantasy over truth. Regardless of the motive in each case, enforcing a gender identity upon a child is tantamount to humiliation. Children are used by adults as a means of insurance, pride and joy. The beliefs and traditions of Afghan culture are so entrenched that they make progress impossible – impossible like passing under a rainbow. Little girls will continue running for it, to pursue the dream of being a boy. And the phenomenon of bachagona posh will continue to perpetuate itself.

Notes

1 Shayestah Wahdat, interview by the author, December 2016.

2 Ibid.

3 Jenny Nordberg, *The Underground Girls of Kabul: in Search of a Hidden Resistance in Afghanistan* (London: Virago Press, 2014), 43–4.

4 Eid is an Islamic holiday, which takes place twice a year. The first occasion marks the end of Ramadan and the second is the Festival of the Sacrifice. Norooz marks the New Year in some parts of the Middle East; it coincides with the 21st of March in the Gregorian Calendar.

5 Wahdat, interview by the author, December 2016.

6 Ibid.

7 Gerda Lerner, *The Creation of Patriarchy* (New York: Oxford University Press, 1986).

8 Jenny Nordberg, *What is a bacha posh?*, Little Digital co., 2014, accessed 18 December 18, 2017, http://bachaposh. com/bacha-posh-2.

9 Ibid., *Bachagona posh* (Darī) means 'dressed like a boy'.

10 Wahdat, interviewed by the author,

December 2016.

11 Nordberg, *The Underground Girls of Kabul*, 61.

12 Abdullah Qazi, *The Plight of the Afghan Woman*, accessed December 20, 2016, www.afghan-web.com/woman.

13 Siddiq Barmak, *Osama* (Afganistan, Ireland, Japan, Iran, Netherlands: Barmak Film, LeBroqcuy Fraser Productions, NHK, 2003).

14 The Golden Age of Afghanistan was the period between 1930 and 1970 when the constitution promoted gender equality and several influences from the West, which turned Afghanistan into the most progressive country in Central Asia. Education, fashion, music and film culture flourished, carrying the promise of a prosperous future. Women were emancipated and able to achieve high positions in government and society.

15 Nordberg, *The Underground Girls of Kabul,* 68–9.

16 Colin Ward, *The Child in the City* (New York: Pantheon Books, 1978), 211.

17 Habiba Amany, in discussion with the author and Shayestah Wahdat, January 2017.

18 Ibid.

19 Ibid.

20 Ibid.

21 Nordberg, *The Underground Girls of Kabul*, 70.

22 Amany, January 2017.

23 Ibid.

24 UNICEF, UN conventions on the Rights of the Child, Article 8, accessed January 10, 2017, www.unicef.org/rightsite/files/uncrcchilldfriendlylanguage.pdf.

25 Wahdat, Interview by the author, December 2016.

26 Sara Ahmed, *A Willfulness Archive* (Durham: Duke University Press, 2014), 2.

27 Nordberg, *The Underground Girls of Kabul*, 98.

28 Ibid., 77.

29 Ibid.

30 Qazi, T*he Plight of the Afghan Woman*.

31 Typical female garment which covers the whole body and culminates in a headscarf.

32 Barmak, *Osama*.

33 Nordberg, *The Underground Girls of Kabul,* 63–4.

34 Ibid., 67.

35 Ibid., 46.

36 Najiba Noorzai, Interview by the author, December 2016.

37 Ibid.

38 Nordberg, *The Underground Girls of Kabul,* 22–3.

39 John Burnett, *Destiny Obscure: Autobiographies of Childhood, Education, and Family from the 1820s to the 1920s* (Hove, UK: Psychology Press, 1982).

40 Nordberg, *The Underground Girls of Kabul,* 17–9.

41 Ibid., 45.

42 Ibid., 24.

References

Ahmed, Sara. *A Willfulness Archive*. Durham: Duke University Press, 2014.

Arendt, Hannah. *The Human Condition* (2nd edition). Chicago: University of Chicago Press, 1998.

Barmak, Siddiq. *Osama*, 2003. Afghanistan: NHK, 2004. DVD.

Bumiller, Elisabeth. *Remembering Afghanistans Golden Age*, 2009. Accessed February 2, 2017. www.nytimes.com/2009/10/18/weekinreview/18bumiller.html.

Burnett, John. *Destiny Obscure: Autobiographies of Childhood, Education, and Family from the 1820s to the 1920s*. Hove, UK: Psychology Press, 1982.

de Certeau, Michel. *The Practice of Everyday Life*, trans. Steven Randall. Berkeley: University of California Press, 1984.

Highmore, Ben. 'Walls without museums: Anonymous history, collective authorship and the document.' *Visual Culture in Britain* 8, no. 2 (2007): 1–20.

Katrin Wahdat

Lerner, Gerda. *The Creation of Patriarchy*.
    New York: Oxford University Press, 1986.
Nordberg, Jenny. *The Underground Girls of
    Kabul: in Search of a Hidden Resistance in
    Afghanistan*. London: Virago Press, 2014.
Nordberg, Jenny. *What is a bacha posh?* Little
    Digital co. Accessed December 18, 2017.
    http://bachaposh.com/bacha-posh-2.
Qazi, Abdullah. *The Plight of the Afghan
    Woman. Afghanistan online*. Accessed
    December 20, 2016. http://www.afghan-
    web.com/woman.
Ward, Colin. *The Child in the City*. New York:
    Pantheon Books, 1978.
Whitlock, Monica. 'Helmand's Golden Age.'
    BBC News. Accessed January 2, 2017.
    www.bbc.co.uk/news/special/2014/
    newsspec_8529/index.html.
UNICEF. *UN conventions on the Rights of the
    Child*, Article 8. Accessed January 10, 2017.
    https://www.unicef.org/rightsite/files/
    uncrcchilldfriendlylanguage.pdf.

Bridge to Kobane: Future Imaginaries and Visual Approaches to Kurdish Migration

Lana Askari, interviewed by Sander Hölsgens

Lana Askari's documentary film *Bridge to Kobane* (2016) tells the story of Mihemed, a Kurdish journalist from the Syrian Kurdish city of Kobane, who lives in a refugee camp in Iraqi Kurdistan. After a nine-month battle with the Islamic State, Kurdish forces liberated Kobane in 2015, making the city a new symbol of Kurdish resistance. Despite the liberation, a return to Kobane remains impossible due to the ongoing war. Connecting Kobane bridge in Sulaimani, Iraqi Kurdistan, to Mihemed's longing for a return to his hometown, the film explores themes of mobility, death and ever shifting horizons in connection with cross-border perceptions of the Kurdish nation.

Migration lends itself to the visual anthropological endeavour. Editing a film mirrors the processual, unstable and fragmented nature of mobility. A quintessentially modern and probably modernist medium, film gestures towards hesitant forms of documentation, fragmented subjectivities, sensory paradoxes and post-conflict architectures in Kurdistan, a conflict-ridden region where migratory practices have been part and parcel of the lives of inhabitants. If we read Kobane not only as a critical event, but also as a symbol imprinted on the city's physical landscape in Sulaimani, what can we learn about how people negotiate the future during precarious times? Filmmaker Sander Hölsgens interviews Lana Askari, the director of *Bridge to Kobane* and researcher at the Granada Centre for Visual Anthropology at the University of Manchester.

Sander Hölsgens   *Bridge to Kobane* sets its tone with an encouraging exclamation by the protagonist, Mihemed: 'If you have a will, you can do anything.' Though at times tender and mournful, he's sanguine about his family's future while they continue residing in Iraqi Kurdistan and later, when they eventually return to his hometown Kobane. How did you get to know Mihemed and his family? What brought you to research in Kurdistan and how did the idea for the film come about?

Lana Askari   I met Mihemed during my fieldwork period in Sulaimani, where I was following the work of an NGO In the refugee camps. My PhD research focused on locals and how young people saw their future in relation to the unstable political and economic situation – Mihemed just stood out from the rest. Being from Kobane and having escaped the Islamic State with his family, he soon shared his incredible life story with me. A journalist himself, Mihemed was, despite the tough job market, committed to continuing his vocational interests, in the meantime supporting his family by working for an NGO. When I told him I wanted to make a documentary film as part of my research he was keen to be part of it. Making the film was very much a collaborative endeavour; had I not met Mihemed, this film would not have been made. After filming an initial master interview, I started visiting him and his family at the camp where they were living. It was beautiful how he performed and narrated his thoughts for the camera as we got to know each other better. At the same time, it was also heartbreaking to see over the course of the year that his future plans to migrate to the West could not be pursued. So, it was only during the process of filming that the idea of the documentary shifted from a mere portrait film to an exploration of how people in Kurdistan negotiate future horizons during precarious times.

Sander Hölsgens   Mobility and displacement are perhaps two of the most intricate and emphatic themes in contemporary anthropology. The 2018 Biennial Meeting of the Society for Cultural Anthropology, for instance, was structured around a myriad of displaced modes of life: 'episodes of profound political upheaval, intensified crises of migration and expulsion, the disturbing specter of climatic and environmental instability, countless virtual shadows cast over the here and now by ubiquitous media technologies.' The conference asked what it means to live and strive in the face of such movements. I wonder how you'd respond to this question, in light of both the filmmaking process of *Bridge to Kobane* and your collaborations with those who had no choice but to leave their dwellings. Specifically, in what ways did these often unwanted forms of mobility affect or shape Mihemed's sense of home and homecoming?

Lana Askari   Even though issues of mobility and displacement have always been part of human life, I think the recent anthropological interest connects them to current debates on temporality. It brings us back to how people, despite precarious contexts, continue to frame hope for their future lives through different means. For example, Mihemed was actively involved in 'making home' in Sulaimani by investing in social relations through his work as a journalist in the city. Also, when the border with Turkey closed, he started to invest a lot of time and effort in upgrading his house in the camp. When his mother passed away, rather than repatriating her body to Syrian Kurdistan, Mihemed buried her in the local graveyard, making that her final home. So his ideas about where home was were shifting. These actions tell us about the continuation of life and sociality during uncertainty, about how human life is lived, which in anthropology has significant comparative value. Recent works, such as Ghassan Hage's research on hope and the feeling that one is always moving somewhere, also point out that these issues do not just exist under precarity.[1] They affect people everywhere, as our understanding of the world is an unstable one. If we follow phenomenological thought, we all have to deal with the fragmented nature of life and how to make sense of these everyday ruptures.[2]

Sander Hölsgens   In *Bridge to Kobane* the whereabouts of Mihemed and his family are poignant. Although residing in a relatively safe region, he still feels he can't simply go wherever he wants. In his words, 'If I was like that bird, I could go anywhere. I wouldn't leave one bit of the world unexplored. I would go everywhere, see how other people live like, if I had wings. I would go to Kobane – that border between Western and Southern Kurdistan would not exist. If I would leave right now, I would arrive in Kobane by evening.' These words seem to me to be the crux of your film, and I wonder if you could share your thoughts on this tender sequence.

Lana Askari   I think this scene illustrates how the camera can bring out imaginative horizons that are part of human life but are usually not brought out into the public domain.[3] We were walking around the refugee camp and stumbled upon graffiti

Lana Askari, *Bridge to Kobane* (UK, 2016). Mihemed working for the food distribution registration in a refugee camp.

on a building, which read 'Kobane.' I think at that moment we both felt the stucked-ness[4] of Mihemed's situation. Being a refugee, he couldn't leave Iraqi Kurdistan to go to Europe, he couldn't return to Syrian Kurdistan, so he would imagine ways of crossing borders, and that's what he shared with us: something not visible or normally brought up in conversation; it was like a thought experiment. I also reflected on this scene, understanding Mihemed's wish not just as a static wish for return. Rather, it was an expression of the need for free movement to counter the forced mobility of displacement.

Sander Hölsgens   As an anthropologist, what role does film-making play in your research? You have the ability to draw out people so it becomes clear what matters to them, via intimate close-ups, amiable editing techniques, and gentle camera movements. Your filmic ethnographies have the capacity to press close to and be conscientious about the most precarious

Lana Askari   59 of situations. Could you perhaps expand on the process of making the film?

Lana Askari   Working with Mihemed taught me a lot about the collaborative and processual dimensions of conducting research. As I filmed and edited, new reflections and analyses about the material surfaced, which I continuously discussed with Mihemed over the phone. So the process continues even after the film is finished. I was happy to receive feedback and questions during screenings of the film which, in light of new events, put the stories *Bridge to Kobane* tells into a different perspective. Filmmaking then adds a methodological aspect to my research because it draws out different types of information during fieldwork. It also adds a communicative aspect, an alternative way of understanding and analysing the ethnography.

Sander Hölsgens   Relatedly, how did you develop your working methods, and to what extent have they informed your relationship with Iraqi Kurdistan and its residents? Do you feel as though your camera has hindered you in any way?

Lana Askari   The camera can work for you! It opens possibilities of engaging with your informants as it has a naturally collaborative aspect. During my fieldwork it gave me access to people and places, and to aspects of life that emerge only from the performative act of being filmed. It is also familiar to people there, it leads to something tangible they can see on a screen. On the other hand, it limits you when you stand behind the camera; you are focused on only certain parts of your visual field. Constantly shifting between shots, you enter a direct editing process that shapes your experience of being in the field. As with any ethnographic endeavour, you cannot focus on everything at once. However, I always struggled during my fieldwork to negotiate this attention – do I look here or there?

Sander Hölsgens   *Bridge to Kobane* opens with a rite of passage – a musical dance in solidarity with those suffering in Western Kurdistan – and ends with an intimate conversation at a displaced graveyard. So the film chronicles both private experiences and cultural histories. As a filmmaker and anthropologist, how do you orient the personal and the shared towards each other? What do individual anecdotes and stories tell us about the broader and precarious situation in Syrian and Iraqi Kurdistan?

Lana Askari   Anthropology is concerned with different scales, and the relation between 'micro' and 'macro.' In making the film, I had both Western and Middle Eastern audiences in mind. While some people might read the film as a narrative that unfolds from the macro (society) to the micro (personal), my guess is that Kurdish audiences do not read these as separate. Critical events – the liberation of Kobane, the Syrian refugee crisis, and the declaration of Northern Syria as autonomous region – are knitted onto people's narrations so they can make sense of their lives. These events, positive or negative, shape their idea of what possible futures exist for them. Placing Mihemed's individual experiences within the broader local geopolitical context helps us understand how new events draw certain horizons nearer or pushes them further away.

Sander Hölsgens   Within the field of visual anthropology film is sometimes portrayed as a medium through which to approximate, capture or even amplify the invisible and the imaginary. There seems to be an emphatic interest in Soviet montage in particular, as a tool to move beyond all that's visible, audible

Lana Askari, *Bridge to Kobane* (UK, 2016). Building Kobane bridge on the city ring road in Sulaimani (top) and Rojava Rally in Sulaimani, Iraqi Kurdistan (bottom).

and tangible. How does the complex process of filmmaking contribute to your rendering and understanding of topics as complex as migration dynamics and future imaginations? And what is the role of montage in *Bridge to Kobane*?

Lana Askari   The issue with *Bridge to Kobane* was that, physically, we could not show the city of Kobane. Over time Mihemed and his family found out that they were not able to make the crossing to Europe, as many other Syrian refugees had. In order to still capture Mihemed's changing self-perception and his reflection of different life paths and futures, the key was to draw these out by effective montage, particularly the placement of the various events, both personal and bigger ones, within the film. To use montage in such a way as to present a certain absence or invisibility through disrupting the normative space of film; then we perceive – through its absence – something that cannot be understood otherwise.[5] Film can capture the fragmentation in human perception, but also incorporate the multiple perspectives and interpretations that continuously shape our consciousness and experience. Montage then reveals/affords new possibilities for open-endedness, by allowing audiences to interpret visual connections and juxtapositions. In *Bridge to Kobane* I tried to engage with how Mihemed imagines different life paths and reflects on them. Through montage and long-term observational filming, we can open up a space for exploring these shifting horizons and possible futures, to understand how people renegotiate plans during times of crisis.

Sander Hölsgens   I'm aware of the other films you've made in the region: Is *Bridge to Kobane* part of a broader enquiry into migration and mobility in Kurdistan? What are your aims for this collection of films?

Lana Askari   Kurdistan is an understudied region that is often only imagined through the media's output of constant war and conflict. I want to counter these stereotypical images of the Middle East by showing through my films that even though precarity is part of life there, people's everyday lives are much more than that. Issues of migration and mobility offer a lens through which we can understand what it means to be human, even in contexts of uncertainty.

Notes

1   Ghassan Hage, 'Waiting Out the Crisis: On Stuckedness and Governmentality,' in *Waiting,* edited by Ghassan Hage, (Carlton, Vic.: Melbourne University Press, 2009), 97–106.
2   Andrew Irving, 'Into the Gloaming,' in *Transcultural Montage,* edited by Christian Suhr and Rane Willerslev (New York and Oxford: Berghahn Books, 2013), 76–95.
3   Vincent Crapanzano, *Imaginative horizons: An essay in literary-philosophical anthropology* (Chicago: University of Chicago Press, 2004).
4   Term by Hage, 2009.
5   Christian Suhr, and Rane Willerslev, eds., *Transcultural montage* (New York and Oxford: Berghahn Books, 2013).

References

Crapanzano, Vincent. *Imaginative horizons: An essay in literary-philosophical anthropology*. Chicago: University of Chicago Press, 2004.
Hage, Ghassan. 'Waiting Out the Crisis: On Stuckedness and Governmentality.' *Waiting*, edited by Ghassan Hage, 97–106. Carlton, Vic.: Melbourne University Press, 2009.
Irving, Andrew. 'Into the Gloaming.' *Transcultural Montage,* edited by Christian Suhr and Rane Willerslev, 70–95. New York and Oxford: Berghahn Books, 2013.
Suhr, Christian, and Rane Willerslev, eds. *Transcultural montage*. New York and Oxford: Berghahn Books, 2013.

A Season
in the Olive Grove

Ektoras Arkomanis

Athens, 6 July 2014

Dear Zoe,
In Eleonas I search for the conscience of my race
manifest only for a brief moment
in the early twentieth century,
or perhaps the nineteenth,
now un-forged, un-created.

Eleonas is marginal, un-metropolitan, entropic – an area near the centre of Athens, with leftover industries, scavengers' markets, shacks and sheds, informal infrastructures, permanent and transitional populations. *Thousands of years ago thousands of olive trees stood here.*

I first encountered Eleonas in a set of photographs that seemed like telltales but at second glance worked against narrative completeness. They depicted dereliction all around, but also people working in defunct factories; flooded roads without pavements and stray dogs in empty streets at twilight, as well as signs of inhabitation and activity like a parked up caravan with a roughly patched-up roof, dyed leather hung to dry between sheds with broken windows, or a framed picture still hanging on the last remaining wall of a demolished house.

Incomplete narratives: first encounter with Eleonas through photographs.

[Take] a gravel road called Ploutonos St. As you make your way, you'll come across Orfeos St. These chthonic names have an ambiguous significance here. Life thrives in this area. And at the same time you get the impression of a landscape that has died: you are in the place where the city banishes all its waste, all that is useless and unwanted.[1]

After the photographs came the official narratives. Two historical images of Eleonas linger on: one from antiquity, when it was the sacred olive grove of Athens (*eleonas* is the Greek word for 'olive grove'), a vast land to the west and southwest of the city, where, according to myth, all the olive trees of Greece are descended from; the other from the late nineteenth and early twentieth centuries, as crops gradually replaced the olive trees. Vine fields and cabbage gardens proliferated, along with small businesses like kilns, tile makers and sack makers; these had first appeared in Eleonas in the late 1820s, after the end of Ottoman rule, aiding the reconstruction of Athens and signaling the eventual replacement of sacred nature with agriculture and industry.

More wholesome stories slowly surfaced, as I was filming, and from the book I was reading, by the ethnographer Zoe E. Ropaitou-Tsaparelli, which contained testimonies by the people of Eleonas, from the 1920s onwards. I continued filming and taking notes for some time, not knowing what I was looking for, only that I wanted to bear witness. By the summer of 2015 the filmed material was pointing towards work – occupations, things that people do. There was often a difficulty in capturing that which you had encountered the previous day – a sense of things migrating before you thought to note them down – because this is not the kind of place that takes interest in its own history. The slow migrations – the transferences of services and the use of land – are interwoven with a long history of migrating populations to Eleonas. None of these migrations have been documented in detail, but their traces are still legible in the urban fabric and in collective memory.

This is a collection of notes about work and migrations, taken as I make the film *A Season in the Olive Grove*, which began in 2014 and is still a work in progress. My film and writing attempt a direct treatment of the place, its people, and the histories contained in its present image. Testimonies, clippings, and excerpts from early twentieth-century literature enter the frame, often distorted, recounted from memory, or filtered through more immediate observations. As people, identities and meaning continue to migrate, as the subject shifts and the ground shifts, two overarching sentiments remain: an uncertainty as to what exactly is preserved or restored by this attentiveness, and the sensation that the stories and images I collect – of things on their way out – more often than not speak of forgetting.

Work

The last remaining tannery, behind Agiou Polykarpou Street, invokes the image of early industry in Eleonas. If two centuries ago the tanners' work was directed towards the nearby city, now it faces inwards – a condition of labour in a globalised economy. The noise of the machines and tools is constant, and the putrescent smell unrelenting. Daylight enters through chinks in the tin roof and walls, and is bolstered by the neon lamps. The rough floor glistens from the regular hosing, sometimes with flashing rainbows of chemicals. Residents and other local businesses are not sympathetic towards the tanneries because of the drainage of toxic chemicals, so the rest of the tanneries in the area closed down some time ago, as did the bone grinder's yard that operated nearby.

The most common tasks are soaking the skin in chemicals, roll-pressing and steam-pressing it, and cutting the edges and loose ends. The soaking is done in huge revolving barrels containing chemicals. Then the skin is inserted into the roll-press, which is operated by foot. The edges of the raw skin are cut manually with long sharp knives. After the skin is pressed each piece is trimmed using scissors. The pressed skins are dyed at another site a couple of blocks away. Most of these tasks are repeated several times, with variations in tools and precision, and there are numerous work surfaces and stations corresponding to the specific stages of treatment – the workers often move along with the production line. On a slow day I counted fifteen men and one woman, all immigrants, but usually there are more.

Between filming trips to Athens I watched Rahul Jain's film *Machines* in a London cinema.[2] Inside a labyrinthine textile sweatshop in Sachin, India, Jain's camera zigzags through corridors, pauses, dwells on machines in vast warehouses, then moves on, discovering tucked-away rooms where people are napping between shifts. Often the camera rests on the colourful, patterned fabrics; this is a spatial as much as temporal punctuation in the film, because these Indian textiles are instantly recognisable from the homes, restaurants, hotels and markets where one finds them, so amid these dull industrial settings they seem imported – brief bursts of colour that re-fragment the interior that the long travelling shots painstakingly assemble.

In the tannery in Eleonas there is no such stark colour contrast, but warm, earthly tones instead: the untreated skin, the aluminum rust, the old unpainted wood and the muddy floors ... when you fix your eyes on a view it begins to resemble an oil painting. The human figures move, slowly, repetitively,

... the city fades from memory: Days of filming and forgetting
in the last remaining tannery in Eleonas.

and over time the scene rearranges itself as though it were recording an old master-painter's reluctance to settle on a composition. Meanwhile, the city fades from memory. *Days of filming. An itch to record, in order to remember and remind. And in the process forgetting, always forgetting ...*

The filmic language of *Machines* became a counter-reference in other ways too: instead of long moving takes, the filming in the tannery demanded static shots that illustrate the slow passage of time from the perspective of the workers, and occasionally a protracted camera pan for observing simultaneous activities or conveying the setting. Then there was the question of what to leave out of the film. Towards the end of Jain's film the focus shifts towards politics, mainly through interviews about the employment conditions inside the factories, the phenomenon of commuting in India (a mass daily migration), exploitation, the diminished rights of the labourers and the repercussions of strike action, which involve intimidation and in some cases even killings. All these circumstances are aspects of working in these sweatshops, rather than the nature of work, which was my preoccupation at the tannery. For this reason there are no interviews, dialogue or voiceover narration, only machine noise.

Words in silence, lists

> So many things had to be learned, and the rules for getting
> ahead bled together in her diary. Sixty percent of people do not
> have a goal. For a look of 'Gorgeous Radiance', blend black,
> grey, golden yellow, sapphire blue, and bright red eye shadow.
> Ⓐ Can be dry-cleaned; 'A' means any detergent can be used.
> The exchange of greetings is the catalyst and lubricant of
> conversation. When you drink soup, don't let the soup spoon

rattle against the plate. People who don't read books will find their speech dull and their appearance repulsive.[3]

I was reading Leslie T. Chang's *Factory Girls: Voices from the Heart of Modern China* at the time, and amid the local realities of work in Chinese factories that the book details, the workers' own diary entries speak most profoundly to the human condition of labour, especially in seemingly trivial moments. Chunming, who is an internal migrant, learns English for personal development, but for those who take up work in foreign countries, learning the language is a necessity. In the tannery and elsewhere in Eleonas I wonder if the workers fill their long silences internally with lists of recently learned Greek words, rehearsing conversations for when their shift is over and they're out in the city buying a snack or bus tickets.

> At one point Chunming decided to learn English on her own.
> She made a list of vocabulary words –
> ABLE
> ABILITY
> ADD
> AGO
> ALWAYS
> AGREE
> AUGUST
> BABY
> BLACK
> BREATH
> – but gave up before she got to C.[4]

Machine noise, aria

There are clues to a world that exists outside the tannery: sometimes you hear the radio when the machines pause, then the slabs of the press begin to move apart again and the radio voices fade into the released steam; or there are brief moments when workers on their way from the main shed to the steam-press warehouse cross an alley under bright sunlight – such as on most days in this part of Europe – a half-forgotten reality for those working inside and, by now, for the viewer of the film. Another sense of the outside world comes from an aged worker as a fact about trade: some of the leather produced here is exported to Italy, to become Gucci, Dolce & Gabbana, etc. Suddenly this smelly shed on the backstreets of Eleonas is a dot on a map, connected to other dots, fashionable designer outlets elsewhere on the continent.

The old man's remark on skin as a commodity unwittingly disentangles skin from everything else, present or distant: the shed, the workers, the conditions of work, the light, the chemicals, D&G – all these are peripheral, ephemeral, perhaps even incidental, whereas the commodity is a constant. Human-kind has traded leather since ancient times. So, in the next sequence everything but the leather gives way. First, the work-ers – we see the same workstations now empty and quiet. The silent interval continues into the cold room where the skin is stored, stacked up in piles. We hear Donizetti's aria *Una Furtiva Lagrima*, together with another, dissonant track. The surround-ings fade too as the camera closes in on piles of sheepskin. As the aria ascends, the other sounds cease – a metaphor for the commodity freeing itself from all that is circumstantial. In the aria's libretto the foolish protagonist spends his last money on a love potion hoping to win his beloved woman's adoration, so the story correlates with the commodification of love, to which leather goods are accessory.

'Have you seen tanneries abroad?', the worker asks me. 'They are mansion halls. Not like this one. Spotless. Museums.'

What you depart from

Athens, 16 April 2015

Dear Zoe,
From the signs in Eleonas I come to know
the ecumene –
Karpenisi, Atalanti, Amfikleia,
Krestena, Zacharo, Gastouni, Vartholomio,
Andravida, Lechaina, Varda,
Almyros,
Itea, Skydra, Aridaea,
Magoula, Mandra,
Megalo Peyko.

More map dots: everywhere in Eleonas the signs of cargo transport companies list their destinations – an exercise in domestic
geography. Like in Whitman's poem-lists, some names half-
obscure their own origin, but not enough to put you off imagining the features they recall: a fruitful island, a salty place, a great
oak. These are but the linguistic residues of the discipline of
geography in an area that has become its own map, mile to mile.
Cargo transport businesses proliferate in Eleonas because
they only need a storehouse and a loading pier. Their shutters
are down most of the time; opening hours are whenever jobs
come along. We set up the camera across the street from a loading pier, outside a car repair garage – another improvised shed –
where two old mechanics are playing cards. 'Eleonas is the
centre of the world,' one of them tells me without lifting his eyes
from the game, as though this were self-evident. We film the
loading and then the lorry departing, then another loading and
another departure. *Engine off, a brief exchange, silent loading,
boxes with unseen contents, signing dockets and getting dockets
signed…* The stations and stops – the dots – are a way of reading

the network, making sense of it, but are also misleading because the long lines that connect the dots represent the true nature of the job. *For hours straight, days on end, the road: motorways, rest stops, gas stations and parking lots, random encounters, checking mileage and delivery schedules, the motorway again, radio on, sat nav, vanishing points and voices.*

Watching departures can have a hypnotic effect; it is comforting to condense the meaning of work into one digestible image of a lorry driving off. Samuel Stevens's film, *Passage*, omits the journeys altogether and instead focuses on cargo ships observed from the shore of the Marmara Sea, and then on lorries at Kapikule, an overland crossing point, from Turkey to Bulgaria, part of a route into and also out of Europe that has existed for centuries.[5] Who is on these ships and who drives these lorries? Ships looking still in the distance, 16-millimetre black-and-white film. Parked lorries, low-contrast black-and-white digital video. This stillness is deliberate because it is necessary. We need these journeys to come to a halt – infinite number of frames per second – and for someone to explain them, even with just one word. The title 'passage' remains on the screen throughout – how else to make sense of this mobile infrastructure and the lives it nourishes, unexamined, on the move but not nomadic?

Precious stone et cetera

Just off the open-air market on Agiou Polykarpou Street, a row of warehouses leads to a mound animated by loaders and excavators purging earth of litter so it can be reused in construction. In Eleonas you grow so used to waste and all sorts of daily contamination that you don't expect to come across preservation of any kind, let alone instances of purification. But about a mile to the east, in Kerameikos, the ancient cemetery of Athens and now a threshold between the city centre and Eleonas, archaeologists and conservators take on cleaning the old stones of the Themistoclean Wall and the ruins of its ancient residential adjuncts. We film close-ups of the repair tool and the restorer's hand. This is a universe of slow frictions: the wearing of stone, moss, shaded recessions and darkened, polluted edges, visible moisture, the tools and toothbrushes that scratch and scrape for months, the glue and the fallen trimmings being fitted back in. With a slow upward pan the camera leaves behind the repairing hand and travels over stone, up the wall. As it looks over the wall, the scene opens up and reveals more walls and ruins, stone on stone, amid more stone, two acres of stone awaiting the same quiet settling of hands on it, a slow and precise endeavour against greater, indiscriminate forces. *Stone turns to sugar.*

Cut to a different kind of preservation, in the scavengers' markets of Eleonas, which stretch for several blocks and feature millions of items, some utterly worthless. Or maybe useless, not worthless, because here the common presumption is that anything can be sold; a 90s Nokia phone charger with its cable cut in half, loose pigeon feathers, an unwashed milk carton – all stubborn refusals to accept that certain things cannot possibly be of value or interest anymore.

Athens, 6 June 2015

Dear Zoe,
One could write an encyclopedia of the rubbish sold in the markets of Eleonas, with tomes like 'Old new technology' or 'Toys', and entries like 'Mutilated *Dora the Explorer* doll'. This book – the encyclopedia that contains the whole market – perhaps exists already and is on sale here, somewhere in the market, but impossible to locate.

Types of preservation: restoration of ancient stone at Kerameikos / re-collected and resold debris of the present at the scavengers' market in Eleonas.

Once I've taken in the variety of merchandise and its degrees of uselessness, the waste at the end of the day strikes me as a paradox. I wonder what sorting criteria are at work here – why sun-melted batteries are discarded, for example, whereas contaminated food containers are deemed fit to sell. Walking around the market I find books from the 1970s with titles such as *World History* or *The History of Mankind: The 20th Century*. Second-hand histories, scavenged, recycled. My mind travels back to Kerameikos and to a treasured ancient artefact found there, the amphora of Dipylon. No one knows for certain what it contained – a void history.

The following day, we film a lone man dressed in rags, inspecting a now empty lot at the scavengers' market site. He is looking for scraps that have escaped all other scavengers and the cleaners. He is the last in the refuse chain, *homo oeconomicus*, holding on to the undignified cetera and feeding them back into this system, which is neither cultural nor natural, but rational in its self-organisation.

The forgetting of work

If you don't know the names, the knowledge of things perishes also.[6] Carolus Linnaeus, *Philosophia Botanica*, 1751, §210

Athens, 30 June 2015

Dear Zoe,

I finished your book this morning. So many words that I didn't know … tools, materials, products, lines of work that no longer exist – lost economies. Ethnography that I prefer to read as though it were the natural history of a vanished ecosystem. The botanist keeps arriving at places where the genera have already disappeared and finds only their names instead.

Soon they too will be forgotten unless she records them.
*Footprints. Philosophia Botanica in reverse. Half-stories
on wet soil. Maybe a name is what gives in last.*

Work passes into memory when the world becomes indifferent
to its offering. At this point in the film, abandoned factories
parade across the screen. Here the format had to differ, to
signify that the subject is not the factory but something less
tangible: the memory of work. Having thought of postcards,
the obvious impulse was to freeze the images, and yet I liked
the idea of postcards not staying still. At times the camera glides
along the street, or there is a shake of the lens because of
the wind on an exposed location – a kind of non-textual anno-
tation. In another universe the filmic postcards would become
synchronous with their subject, recording the wear of the
factories and the change of seasons, and perpetually renewing
the film. In this world, their short stretch – a few seconds on
film – is followed by a notional expansion once the idea has
taken root in the viewer's mind.

Invented memories
In the film, the memory of work is a constructed one; neither
the filmmaker nor the audience had been inside the factories
while they were still operational. My actual memories have
formed from advertisements of these companies on TV and on
billboards ranging along the motorway we drove through every
summer to get out of Athens. To a child, those advertisements
made the companies ubiquitous – Petalouda made the threads
and needles of the world. Now, looking at their empty factories
I realise it's not nostalgia that I'm experiencing but a collapse
of temporalities – reading outdated warnings about the fate of
these companies *after* it has arrived.

The Athenian Paper Company (Athinaiki Hartopoieia) was founded in the 1930s, and at its peak employed two-and-a-half thousand workers. By 2014, when I began filming, it had already experienced several misfortunes and had shrunk to half that number of employees. We drove between the tall wall of its empty warehouse on one side of the street and a burned compound with a series of units and yards on the other. Halfway through, an overhead transporter bridge joins the two buildings, as if tracing the history of disasters from fire, over the street, to bankruptcy. It felt strange that there was still work amid these ruins. The street sign reads Paperworkers' Street – a lexical remnant amid the material ones from a time when work thrived here, a reminder of a collective future that was once discernible, for a brief time almost tangible.

There was yet another fire around that time, and then, in 2016, the company finally succumbed to its fate. I was filming elsewhere in Eleonas when I read about this, and instead of a moment of clarity when the end of a story lets you make sense of it, there was the sensation that the film itself was becoming a ruin. With the last workers now gone, these factories, whittled away by calamities and preserved in their desolate state by an unravelled national economy, became legible, perhaps on the whole poignant, but up-close meaningless.

The postcard shots were then separated by blackout screens – a further ruination of the film – and machine noise, which implies that work ceased only recently in most of these factories. This involves two discontinuities, one temporal and one spatial: we see the exteriors of the buildings but we hear sounds from the *inside*, and *from another time*, presumably not long ago. The effect is illusory, a kind of filmic seashell resonance: the machine noise was recorded elsewhere and artificially overlaid, to complete the invented memory. Does this make the film complicit in the forgetting of work?

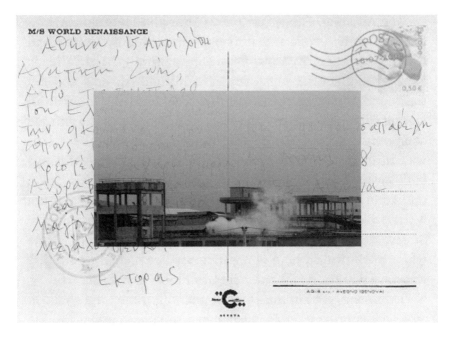

Postcards from Eleonas: screen postcard with a moving image inlay that shows smoke coming out of the Athenian Paper Company's factory, a few months before its final closure.

In the last shot of a factory, smoke comes out of its chimney. The filmed circumstance is real, so the image can be read as a triumphant regaining of function. But I prefer to see it as the last stage of delusion, when reality is stored away as false memory.

Labours of the months and years
A cluster of abandoned buildings that once was a cement sales company is now a series of concrete frames in dusty hues, outlined against the sky and surrounded by pools of undrained water. *Empty streets and piazzas, 15th-century ideal cities, after the celebrations, after the rain. Pittura metafisica. Antonioni.* A little rise, which curves around the cluster of buildings, terminates at an unplanned viewing platform. From up here a rift

'Anthills': Abandoned site of a cement sales company – an example of the type of views in Eleonas that become internalised.

between the foreground and background opens up, in bird's eye view, like in a Bruegel painting, so I begin to mentally populate the scene with hundreds of characters – perhaps from the nearby markets – labouring away in uncomfortable positions, remaining indifferent to one another's activities and concerns as days go by, seasons change and nature gradually reclaims the site. *Babel. Children's Games. Anthills.*

Like a Prayer / Contempt
In the front yard of a sculptor-potter's workshop we find hundreds of clay replicas of ancient statues. I'm drawn to the ones that come in groups; some Pans and a dozen caryatids lined up as small armies – unintended visions of subdued individuality. The artist tells us that he once received an order (which was later cancelled) for more than a hundred statuettes for the parapets of a villa that Madonna, the pop star, wanted to build on a Greek island. The purported intention was that the whole villa would rotate throughout the day to otherworldly lighting effect, a.k.a. Ciccone dazzle. In the workshop's front yard there are also statues of ancient gods, as you'd expect, and filmed against the ash-blue sky their eyes look even more vacant than usual – which is perhaps the contrast that gave Godard the idea to airbrush them with light blue or ceramic-red hues in one of the rare instances of scrutiny that ancient Greek artefacts have endured on film.[7]

Athens, 14 March 2016

Dear Zoe,
When antiquity departed from Eleonas it left behind small clusters of fake jewels, cheap souvenirs scattered amid the sweatshops and the ruins.

Perhaps this is the legacy of the statues' empty stare: the story of a nation that, consumed by its ancient history, forgot its more recent past. There are many signs and symbols in Eleonas that point to antiquity: Iera Odos (The Sacred Way), to begin with, which in classical times connected Athens to the town of Eleusis in the west, and was the trail of the Eleusinian Mysteries, the preeminent rite in the ancient Greek world. Today it's a modern avenue that runs an almost identical course with its ancestor: it begins from Kerameikos, cuts through Eleonas and leads to the western suburbs. One night I notice a few miniature trains that take tourists on amusement rides around the Acropolis; they are being refueled here, at a gas station on Iera Odos – nowadays more infrastructure than venerable site – and then parked up at the back, where they reside.

Across the road, in a little recess edged with stone, stands Plato's Olive Tree (no recorded connection to Plato, though the tree is at least as old). Or *stood*, rather, up until the mid-1970s, when a bus drove right into it. The tree survived that impact too, and was transferred a few hundred metres down the road to the agriculture university for first aid and a second, sheltered life, while another olive tree was transplanted on the spot as a stand-in.

After the double of Plato's Olive Tree and some more 'Iera Odos' road signs, we find a façade of a packaging products manufacturer, with pediments on the three entrances, duly accessorised with volutes in gaudy colours, while the rest of the building is carried out in plain factory vernacular. Over time, I have developed some affection for these kitch jewels because they suit the present entropy of Eleonas. They are casually embedded in the landscape and speak to the constant migration of meanings, which is the broader narrative of my film and this essay.

Memories of land and swimming, labour and fruits

Searching for the late nineteenth and early twentieth centuries, we find an imposing two-storey farmhouse, set back from Orfeos Street and hidden from view by a surrounding wall. It dates back to that time when the olive trees in Eleonas gave way to vine crops, cabbage gardens and vineyards. We climb over the wall to look at the old ruin and imagine how it was to have land worked by others. *Muscat vineyards, sorrow-less life.*[8] There are no crops left now; a wild field covered in July-platinum hay surrounds the ruin. *Faenum. The land forgets too.* At the edge of the field someone has tied three horses. *If my neighbour is idle, incapable of cultivating his land, then I'm not sinning if I trespass on it.*[9] Nearby there is an empty trough, the size of a small room, built of large plinths. 'There were troughs in the crop fields, countless troughs, and windlass wells. In the troughs we learned how to swim, wearing trunks that our mothers made for us from sugar sacks.'[10]

Remains of a two-storey farmhouse that dates back to the early-twentieth or late-nineteenth century, when agriculture thrived in the area.

A Season in the Olive Grove

12 Knossos Street (*Unsung, unmourned*)

Knossos Street doesn't look ancient, let alone Minoan; it is just another narrow, winding street in Eleonas that heavy-duty lorries regularly pass through. A couple of sheds with kilns for smelting batteries were built here in the 1970s, but never came to function, not as intended anyway. An old metallurgist who was brought in at the time to supervise the project now uses the site to smelt metals that he'd rather not name, because it's an illegal activity. He holds the last specialist degree of its kind from the national polytechnic university. He recounts laws banning the burning of various metals over the last half-century, and claims that these laws have always corresponded to the demands or oversaturation of the market, rather than to environmental sensibilities. He limps a bit but is eager to demonstrate how he pours the liquefied metal. He doesn't want to be filmed doing the real thing, so he just goes through the motions, shovelling air from an empty bucket and pouring it into an empty tray. No fiery matter, no names – everything is missing from this image.

Athens, 18 March 2016

Dear Zoe,
I saw Hephaestus today, at Knossos St. *Onto one flame, another.* He limps ever since his father tossed him from the sky and he crashed onto the island of Limnos. I peaked into his furnace – it has gone cold. *Onto one sorrow, another.*

We return a year later, and he's limping badly, he can no longer work by himself and is waiting for 'the kid' that helps him. Maybe the kid will show up later today; if not, then tomorrow. Another year goes by and we never see him again; whenever we happen by, the gate is locked and his car not there. I often wonder what became of him, the last artificer to leave this land, whose face I once glanced at here, in Eleonas.

The perpetual migration

The history of displacements of functions and services, the shifts in the identity of the place and the perennial deferrals of meaning would not follow the same course or have the same poignancy were it not for the migrations of people to Eleonas that have occurred over the past century.

The refugee camp in Eleonas is a grid of prefabricated human containers and the aisles or passageways between them – a spatial order laid over the temporal uncertainty in the life of its inhabitants. Looking down the aisles offers a respite from human traffic and visual information, and so the various

Typical passage between containers in the Eleonas refugee camp. The variation in these homogenous spaces is owed to the human element and to signs of inhabitation (the protruding hand of a man smoking out of the window, a washing line, discarded items, etc.).

A Season in the Olive Grove

histories of immigrants in Eleonas revisit me all at once, legible on everyday items like pushchairs, buckets and brooms, old suit-cases, cheap boxes and shoes, which come into relief against the whiteness of the containers.

Exchangeables

In the early 1920s a million-and-a-half Greeks fled from Turkey following the mutual atrocities between the two states, which culminated in a population exchange in 1923. Around 300,000 of refugees arrived in Athens and settled mostly on the western fringes of the city in places like Eleonas, uninhabited or severely underdeveloped. They became known as 'the exchangeables,' a name used by press and populace alike as debates over 'what to do' with them, where to accommodate them, etc. dominated the headlines in the following years and turned this into the most divisive socio-political issue of the time. Two dilapidated adobe-brick houses at either end of Orfeos Street recall that mass migration, which saw Eleonas demoted from an outskirt to a fringe where the city banishes the people and things it would rather not see.

'I am a Turk,' Mr Yiannis says to introduce himself. His native language is Greek; he's in his late sixties and works in a warehouse overseeing lorry arrivals, loadings and departures. During the interwar period the dourest antipathy was directed towards Muslim Greeks who had been chased out of Turkey because of their Greek nationality, and were looked down upon in Greece because of their Muslim faith. They were referred to simply as 'Turks,' an identity label which they gradually adopted themselves, realising they would forever be outcasts in this society too. Mr Yiannis tells us that they organise their kin's weddings in abandoned sheds in Eleonas – the last one took place two nights ago. They lay out tables and benches brought from their homes and workplaces, eat and dance until late, then clean up and leave the place as they found it, even if it belongs to them and no one else is likely to set foot there.

Over the last three decades a steady migration of Kurdish people has taken place mainly from Iraq and, to a lesser extent, from Turkey. Kurds are today one of the most accepted minorities in Greek society, but this was not the case early on. Back in the 1980s only a small number sought asylum while most thought it safer to remain as unseen as possible.

> We live here, ten Kurdish families. Thirty people. We are Muslims. We don't have water or electricity. Our children don't go to school. We're always afraid because we don't have permits. Some are scavengers, others work in construction sites, another works in a petrol station, some don't have work. We have good relationships with people, we have no complaints. We have Greek names too, to make things easier.[11]

In the late 1980s and throughout the 1990s more than half a million Albanian economic migrants arrived in Greece, and smaller numbers from Romania, Bulgaria, Russia, Ukraine, Armenia and Georgia. These immigrants and their descendants are the workforce of the sweatshops, markets and transportation companies in Eleonas. The long-term exclusion of Eleonas from the official city plan has meant that the industrialisation of the area from the 1960s onwards went hand in hand with all kinds of self-licensing by business proprietors, and with the rampant exploitation of unregistered immigrants in particular.

A few hundred metres to the south of the refugee camp there's an enclave closed off on most sides, hidden from the streets around it and accessible only through a small path between buildings off Orfeos St. Here, a Roma community of about four hundred members, half of them children, had lived for some time within half an acre of land, without water or electricity. Most of them were from Albania and were drawn to Eleonas because they could find work in the markets and scrapyards around and keep a low profile. Ironically, the headquarters of the Attica Foreigners Division, where immigrants have to register and get their papers, is just down the road, forming a geographical triangle with the refugee camp and the Roma camp. Even though a lot of the Roma kids give school a try, they usually drop out very early, either because they're needed for work by their families, or out of shame for not having clean clothes like the rest of the kids.

Over the last decade there had been many complaints by the residents and businesses of Eleonas about the Roma stripping cables from utility poles and then burning them to extract metal – a highly polluting activity. The owners of some local scrap yards were not only perpetuating this by buying the metal

A caravan parked up on an empty lot in spring 2014. A year later the Eleonas refugee camp was set up on the site, and some of the immigrants that lived there had to move elsewhere.

from the Roma and selling it on, but also often initiating it, by stripping and supplying the cables themselves and supplying them to the Roma. In the mid-2010s the government and local authorities ordered the evacuation of the site; some of its inhabitants were relocated to other camps to the east, others dispersed into the neighbouring areas.

Bare life

The history of migration in Eleonas reaches the present with the current movement from Syria and elsewhere in the Middle East, via Turkey, to Aegean islands like Samos and Limnos. Some refugees are transported to Athens and end up in the Eleonas camp. From here they venture out into the city and then continue north to the rest of the continent. An inhabitant of the camp tells me that it took him ten attempts and two years to get here. He begins the story mid-journey, somewhere along the coast of Turkey:

> They sent us to an olive grove near the sea and asked us to stay there until the morning. At six they brought the boat and told us to get in. We were seventy people, we had twenty-five or thirty children on the boat. After ten or fifteen minutes you can't see anything else – sky and water. The sea and the sky, nothing else.[12]

Such are the stories from the refugee camp. They begin in remote places where sovereign law and power cannot be exercised, and yet their consequences are strongly felt. They speak to Giorgio Agamben's concept of 'bare life' – biological life exposed to peril as a result of the politics of modern nation-states. Agamben's *Homo sacer* – a person included in the nation-state but only in the form of an exception – is embodied by the modern refugee as inhabitant of the camp, a spatially defined zone.[13] The refugees in the Eleonas camp are, however, free to come and go at will; they remain here until they feel ready to continue their journey.

Merry Christmas Mr Agamben
Every now and then someone comes out of a container; a man hangs out the laundry to dry, another one repairs a bike. Some do their morning exercise – often for lack of other pasttime activities, you sense. A few months later, while editing, I notice three boys who appear several times in the footage: early morning, roaming around the camp before anyone else is up, with an air of ownership, as if they're inspecting the place, looking to see what has changed, who has moved out, etc.; later, gathering at a corner and briefly conferring, as if exchanging reports on the last few hours, then dispersing again; in the afternoon, running down the aisles, visible in the distance for only a few seconds, before disappearing again behind the containers.

The lessons taking place in the camp school – a covered outdoor space that resembles a canteen, with painted walls and music always playing – are brief and perhaps less oppressive than in state school. Kids enjoy a certain freedom in the camp, but as in most places, this more often applies to boys than girls. A girl comes out of a container carrying a bucket, heading somewhere to fill it up. There is a poem by Pasolini in which adversity cannot subdue the sacred laughter of girls. Coincidentally, the poem is about Athens but, like when you walk through the refugee camp, Athens quickly becomes other places.

In the time of Athens
the girls would laugh in the doorways of squat little houses
    all the same

(as in the poor quarters of Rio)
houses along avenues filled, at the time,

with the fragrance (you couldn't remember the name) of
lindens.

...

It's wartime; and if the girls laugh, it's because they are holy.[14]

A red-hooded girl, five or six years old, wanders around pur-
poselessly, hands in pockets; she looks into the camera for
a few seconds, with unchanging expression, then dawdles on.
It is Christmas Eve, and witnessing first-hand the everydayness
in the refugee camp softens whatever thoughts I have after
reading Agamben. There is calm and a sense of precious life
being slowly reconstituted. Perhaps the camp is a live essay on
the primordial instinct to systematise life so as to protect it, as
events in the world outside become harder to influence or pre-
dict. The spatial arrangement does not narrate anything else
in particular, and so its formal order does not obscure the
inhabitants' tales of peril and perseverance. Still, these tales
would remain fragments – a testimony from the Syrian guy in
container xx, the story of the family living in xy, etc. – with no
connection to one another if not for the kids, whose wanderings
through the camp thread together people, spaces and events.
Meanwhile, the kids' presence alone speaks to the hereditary
problem of assimilation, and to our attitudes towards the marginal and the marginalised.[15]

Epilogue: Easter in Eleonas

Athens, 14 April 2017 (Good Friday)
From the rooftop of an abandoned building the camera pans
across tin roofs, antennas, cables and utility poles, factory shells

and construction yards – there are no olive trees left in Eleonas. A voice from a hundred years ago narrates:

> Observe in the olive grove, which your position reveals as a big thicket; wherever there's a clearing, discern the olive trees, one by one. Each tree of Attica is of distinguished countenance.[16]

Athens, 15 April 2017 (Holy Saturday)

She came from the sunbaked end of the street, a woman in her fifties, carrying blocks of wood, chortling – 'And then they tell you that the man provides for the family.' She stayed for a while and talked to us about her son. The mothers of Eleonas are Balkan, Roma, Middle-Eastern, North African, Indian, Somali, Armenian, Eritrean, Kurdish, Anatolian. The mothers of Eleonas are Mediterranean, with dark hair and big dark eyes, descended from mountain villages, nurtured by islands,

One of the few remaining olive trees in Eleonas. Metal cutters' and some other small workshops were operating in this dead-end neighbourhood until recently, but they were eventually abandoned after repeated looting.

mothers of all the Athens past, mothers of this here Athens. There are cities lost inside them, waiting to be born.

It's Holy Saturday, and from the loudspeakers of the Agios Polykarpos Church the Vespers resound through the neighbourhoods of Eleonas – through the church's vineyard, the agricultural university and the Sacred Way to the north, the refugee camp and the valley with the dumped metals to the west. The land around the farmhouse has turned a lush green with scatters of poppies, daisies and chamomiles, and the horses have run loose ... we come across them at a traffic light nearby. A few cars and passers-by have come to a standstill and look on, wondering where these horses came from.

> Dear Zoe,
> We took a wrong turn and discovered another hidden
> neighbourhood, at a dead end behind the farmhouse field,
> with metal cutters' workshops and bamboos. And we saw
> olive trees for the first time, after three years in Eleonas.
> Olea Europaea sylvestris,
> Bambusoideae,
> Papaver rhoeas
> Anthemis maritima – FF
> If the wrong turn brought us here, why should we always strive
> to stay on the right path?

Athens, 16 April 2017 (Easter Sunday)
In Eleonas there's a contiguity of human elements with nature, on sites that remind you of the urban peripheries in Pasolini's films: dusty streets in mid-afternoon, back yards with flower pots in supermarket trolleys, rooftops with climbers growing around satellite dishes, a small patch of land cordoned off with cassette tape that glints as it sways, perfect for a moment. The scenes you witness lend themselves to the kind of poetry

that sees the eternal in the gritty. It is evening, and immigrant children play football in an alley, next to orange trees and piled up rubbish that together give off that recognisable Mediterranean scent, both sacred and profane. At times these scenes take up writing the film themselves, away from my intentions, narrating how we live in a world that just is.

Acknowledgements

The postcards, though they were never sent, are addressed to the ethnographer Zoe E. Ropaitou-Tsapareli, whose book on Eleonas revealed to me an Athens I knew very little about. I thank her for providing me with a copy of her research on the neighbouring areas of Rouf-Votanikos and Gazi, and especially for turning up in person, one evening in Athens, to hand it over. I thank Serafeim Arkomanis for the walks, conversations and filming in Eleonas; my unnamed informant at the Eleonas refugee camp, and the volunteers and workers of the camp for their assistance; the archaeologist Leonidas Bournias for enabling the filming at Kerameikos and the conservators for participating in the film; Punya Sehmi and Aleks Catina for their valuable reflections on this essay.

Notes

1   Zoe E. Ropaitou-Tsapareli, *Ο Ελαιώνας της Αθήνας: Ο Χώρος και οι Άνθρωποι στο Πέρασμα του Χρόνου.* [Eleonas of Athens: The Space and the People with the Passage of Time.] (Athens: Philipotis, 2006), 136. Original excerpt from: Rania Kloutsinioti, 'Ο Ελαιώνας να γίνει ανάσα ζωής' [Make Eleonas a breath of life], *ANTI*, no. 377 (July 1988), 27–41. Author's translation.

2   Rahul Jain, *Machines* (India, Germany, Finland: Jann Pictures, Pallas Film, IV Films, 2016).

3   Leslie T. Chang, *Factory Girls: Voices from the Heart of Modern China* (London: Picador, 2009), 61.

4   Ibid.

5   Samuel Stevens, *Passage* (2007), accessed 21 November, 2019, www.samuelstevens.co.uk/films.html.

6   'Nomina si nescis, perit et cognitio rerum'. Karine Chemla, Renaud Chorlay and David Rabouin, ed., *The Oxford Handbook of Generality in Mathematics and the Sciences* (Oxford: Oxford University Press, 2016), 264.

7   Jean-Luc Godard, *Le Mépris* [Contempt] (France/Italy: Rome Paris Films, Les Films Concordia, Compagnia Cinematografica Champion, 1963).

8   Alexandros Papadiamantis, *Αμαρτίας φάντασμα* [Ghost of sin] (1900) Εταιρεία Παπαδιαμαντικών Σπουδών [Papadiamantis Studies Organisation], accessed November 21, 2019, http://papadiamantis. net. Author's translation.

9   Ibid. Author's translation.

10 Ropaitou-Tsapareli, 210. Testimony by Pavlos Baltzoglou, resident of Eleonas. Author's translation.

11 Ibid., 322. Veli Rabi Asari, resident of Eleonas, c. 2006 (the precise date of the interview is unknown). Author's translation.

12 Unnamed informant in the Eleonas refugee camp, interview by author, Athens, 24 December, 2017.

13 Giorgio Agamben, *Homo Sacer: Sovereign Power and Bare Life* (Stanford: Stanford University Press, 1998), 4–8, 76–80.

14 Pier Paolo Pasolini, James Ivory and Stephen Sartarelli, *The Selected Poetry of Pier Paolo Pasolini. A Bilingual Edition* (Chicago: University of Chicago Press, 2014), 392–4. From the poem 'Atene' [Athens] (1971).

15 Ektoras Arkomanis, 'Passage Variations: an elliptical History of Migration in Eleonas,' *Architecture and Culture 7*, no. 1 (2019), 109.

16 Periklis Giannopoulos, *Ἑλληνικὴ Γραμμή* [Greek Line] (1900), accessed November 21, 2019, https://pheidias.antibaro.gr Giannopoulos/book-gramme.html. Author's translation.

References

Agamben, Giorgio. *Homo Sacer: Sovereign Power and Bare Life*. Stanford: Stanford University Press, 1998.

Arkomanis, Ektoras. 'Passage Variations: An Elliptical History of Migration in Eleonas,' *Architecture and Culture 7*, no. 1 (2019): 95–111.

Chang, Leslie T. *Factory Girls: Voices from the Heart of Modern China.* London: Picador, 2009.

Chemla, Karine. Renaud Chorlay and David Rabouin, ed. *The Oxford Handbook of Generality in Mathematics and the Sciences.* Oxford: Oxford University Press, 2016.

Giannopoulos, Periklis. Ἑλληνικὴ Γραμμή [Greek Line]. 1900. Accessed November 21, 2019. https://pheidias.antibaro.gr/ Giannopoulos/book-gramme.html.

Godard, Jean-Luc. *Le Mépris* [Contempt]. 1963; France/Italy: Rome Paris Films, Les Films Concordia, Compagnia Cinematografica Champion.

Jain, Rahul. *Machines.* 2016; India / Germany / Finland: Jann Pictures, Pallas Film, IV Films.

Papadiamantis, Alexandros. Ἁμαρτίας φάντασμα [Ghost of sin]. 1900. Εταιρεία Παπαδιαμαντικών Σπουδών [Papadiamantis Studies Organisation]. Accessed November 21, 2019. http://papadiamantis. net.

Pasolini, Pier Paolo, James Ivory and Stephen Sartarelli. *The Selected Poetry of Pier Paolo Pasolini. A Bilingual Edition.* Chicago, IL: University of Chicago Press, 2014.

Ropaitou-Tsapareli, Zoe E. Ο Ελαιώνας της Αθήνας: Ο Χώρος και οι Άνθρωποι στο Πέρασμα του Χρόνου [Eleonas of Athens: The Space and the People with the Passage of Time]. Athens: Philipotis, 2006.

Stevens, Samuel. *Passage.* 2007. Accessed November 21, 2019. www.samuelstevens. co.uk/films.html.

From Exile to Entropy: Notes on Protagonists and the Posthistorical

Sasha Litvintseva

1989 was the year history ended, allegedly. The notion of the posthistorical condition was proposed in the aftermath of the world political events of 1989, and perhaps we can indeed think of that year as a symbolic end, but not in the victory-of-capitalism sense that Francis Fukuyama intended it.[1] In *We Have Never Been Modern*, Bruno Latour points to the double significance of the year 1989: on the one hand it saw the fall of the Berlin Wall, and as such the beginning of the end of socialism; on the other hand it saw the first conferences on the global state of the planet, climate and environment, and as such the beginning of our awareness of the limits of progress.[2] 'The perfect symmetry between the dismantling of the wall of shame and the end of limitless Nature is invisible only to the rich Western democracies,' which, unlike the socialist states that 'destroyed both their peoples and their ecosystems,' have 'been able to save their peoples and some of their countrysides by destroying the rest of the world.'[3] History ended in 1989 in a geologically inspired sense, through which Robert Smithson suggested leaving 'the gardens of history' for experiences of time itself: experiences of material temporality and finitude.[4]

1989 was the same as the year I am writing this, calendrically speaking. Meaning, the dates and days of the week line up the same way across the whole of 1989 and 2017. Perhaps we could get out our diaries from 1989 and use them as almanacs? Is history about to end again, or is it about to start again, or has it never stopped, or has it never been? Calendars themselves are geographically and historically contingent constructions, not translations of cosmic absolutes. The number of months and of days in a single month has fluctuated throughout the history of human civilisation, and the Gregorian calendar – currently in use as standard – is merely hundreds of years old, and was only adopted in most of the non-Western world in the 20th century; this is to say nothing of the days of the week. In 2017 we are seeing ongoing environmental and societal collapse, from continuing wars and the refugee crisis to the resurgence of the far right in Western democracies, all of which are expected to worsen in line with climate catastrophes including increasing droughts, typhoons, forest fires, and drowning shorelines. We are seeing the depletion of fossil fuels lead not to the pursuit of alternative fuels, but pursuit of fossil fuels by ever more expensive and ecologically devastating means. We are seeing the acidification of the oceans and the sixth great extinction; we are seeing population growth, and diminishment of arable lands. The political events of 2017 are likely to propagate violent denialism rather than a search for solutions. In March of that year, Prime Minister Theresa May signed the letter triggering Article 50 of the Lisbon treaty, beginning the process of taking the UK out of the EU on the very same day that US President Donald Trump signed an order undoing Obama-era climate change policies. The political events of the past years are likely to propagate violent denialism rather a search for solutions. A friend recently quipped: 'History has started again: somebody make it stop!'

1989 was the year *Back to the Future Part II* came out: a return to a return to a realm of non-linear time. 21 October 2015 – the date envisioned as the future back in 1989 – is now our past, and the real 21 October 2015 was not as futuristic as anticipated. As per an internet listicle: we still need roads; there are no flying cars; traffic is still terrible, car companies are still claiming it isn't; food waste may be able to serve as a fuel source in experimental contexts but is not being pursued in practice; we have no time machine to speak of yet. Motor vehicles, their terrain, and the power that propels them rule the imaginary. In the then-USSR, my mother, pregnant with me, watched contraband copies of 80s Hollywood films on VHS. These tapes, with an atrocious monotone and off-tempo Russian dubbing – extremely nasal sounding due to being recorded with the nose being held shut so as to render the voice to be untraceable – were copied and passed around at covert meetings in subway stations on early weekend mornings. Cultural imaginaries had the power to shape the future. 2017 would see the remakes of such classics as *Ghost in the Shell*, *Sleeping Beauty*, *Bladerunner* and *Jumanji*; revivals of such seemingly finished franchises as *Alien*, *Star Wars* and *King Kong*; continuations of the never-ending *Pirates of the Caribbean*, *Planet of the Apes* and *The Fast and the Furious franchises*, and resurrections of such characters as Wonder Woman, Spiderman, the Power Rangers and King Arthur. All this in one year. 'The future is only knowable by its difference from the present and the past': what a time to be alive.[5]

1989 was the year I was born. I was born in January above the Arctic Circle: tilt of the Earth's axis meant that for the first two months of my life I didn't see sunlight. I was born in a small residential settlement for the workers of the Kola Nuclear Power Plant in the European far north of the then-USSR, where my father worked as an engineer and my mother as an accountant. My mother jokes that she's relieved I have teeth. My parents moved to this remote and barren place straight after finishing university in Moscow, as working in adverse conditions was then the only way to get paid a little more than the standard wage. My mother's own parents were Soviet geologists, the profession that was considered the most romantic back in the 1950s, with all the songs by the fire during camping trips to Siberia to look for deposits of natural resources. My father's parents were metallurgists, and I'm told my grandfather invented an important aluminium alloy but did not get to keep the patent. After the Soviet Union collapsed, all the money my parents had managed to save was lost to devaluation, and they moved down to Moscow to try and make sense of the new county they suddenly found themselves in. My mother ended up working in the natural resource sector that made this transition to capitalism possible: oil.

I do not say all this to situate myself as, somehow, exceptionally equipped to speak to the entanglement of history and politics with energy and materials, but rather to point to the entanglement itself, and to our necessary and individual enmeshment in it. As an artist and an academic, and in the spirit of Donna Haraway, I am committed to being accountable for the position from which I speak.[6] In this essay I will take this one step further to extrapolate some autobiographical episodes toward a speculative proposition. I will speak to two defining moments of my life, both of which tangentially touch much larger defining moments in the history of the Russian and global entanglement of politics and energy. One of these events took place before I was born, the other is a rupture that split my life into two halves. Each of them forms the seed of a film I have made in recent years, and that I will discuss here. We need to go forward to go back: it is the latter event with which I will begin.

In 2003 the then-wealthiest man in Russia – and head of the country's biggest oil company – was arrested on charges of fraud, and the assets of the company were seized under tax charges. The legitimacy of the case has since been taken up by the European Court of Human Rights, and Amnesty International considers him a prisoner of conscience. The company was initially formed as part of the privatisation of state assets during the 1990s. The arrest and the events that followed essentially reversed the process of privatisation, returning the oil fields and refineries to state control and forming the basis for the foundation and expansion of Gazprom, currently Russia's biggest oil company (a state company unofficially under Putin's control). In the year that followed the initial arrest, and in the calamity of the transition, a tragically high and seemingly arbitrary number of company employees got caught in the crossfire. Some of them were detained, tried and even jailed. My mother was one of them. In our life it was a year that was filled with uncertainty, and ended in exile.

My mother's exile began as an exotic vacation. After her first encounter with the prosecution, she was fortunate enough to be advised to leave the country. However, international travel for Russians was contingent on complicated tourist visas to all but a handful of countries – among these Egypt and Thailand. This is where she fled to when she had to leave suddenly. In the very early spring she found herself to be one of the only customers at a large hotel by the Red Sea. The sea too cold yet for swimming, she wandered the hotel's halls for a month. Later she travelled around rural Thailand, hoping that being on the move would conjure a future into being. The temporality tourism engenders is always suspended, superimposed with the existing flows of the spaces it invades: the circular time of seasons and days, and the linear time of history and daily life. In the case of my mother's enforced vacation this was particularly acute.

In the absence of a future to travel towards, time would not pass. To pass the time, she was drinking piña coladas, while the horizon of the future and the horizon of hope began to resemble a precipice.

The philosopher and media theorist Vilém Flusser was many times an exile. A Czech Jew, he fled the Nazi occupation of Prague as a nineteen-year-old, spending most of his adult life in Brazil and only returning to Europe in the 1970s after what he describes as the failure of the Brazilian project. A polyglot who wrote in four languages (Portuguese, German, English, and French) Flusser theorised the condition of exile and what he called 'homelessness.' In his essays on their generative potential he mixes autobiography and speculation liberally: it is to these texts that I turned when trying to find the right voice for this essay. Indeed I will turn to Flusser at a number of the upcoming junctures of this text, for although I made the films I discuss here before my encounter with his writing, I have inadvertently – almost uncannily – trodden down many of the same paths he had, and now deliberately invoke him as a companion in thought. All of his essays that I mobilise to speak to my own work and experience were written in the late 1980s and early 1990s, and my retroactive inspiration with his ideas can perhaps become another plane on which that time period can converse with the now.

Flusser argues that a disruption of dependable futurity, such as that experienced by those expelled, is in fact generative, creative, and radical. He writes that, having left Prague in flight from the Nazis, he 'felt that the universe was crumbling,' but that it was only after he learned to disassociate his subjectivity from the place to which he was rooted – something only possible through expulsion – he 'realized, painfully, that these now severed attachments had bound' him, leaving him 'overcome by that strange dizziness of liberation and freedom.'[7]

The rootlessness, bottomlessness, groundlessness, and homelessness, as he refers to it, lifts the blanket of habit that covers the facts of life in customary surroundings. In 'Exile and Creativity' he writes:

> Whoever lives in a home finds change informative but
> considers permanence redundant. In exile, everything is
> unusual. Exile is an ocean of chaotic information. In it,
> the lack of redundancy does not allow the flood of information
> to be received as meaningful messages. Because it is unusual,
> exile is unlivable. One must transform the information
> whizzing around into meaningful messages, to make it livable.
> One must 'process' the data. It is a question of survival:
> if one fails to transform the data, one is engulfed by the waves
> of exile. Data transformation is a synonym for creation. The
> expelled must be creative if he does not want to go to the dogs.[8]

As everything around the expelled becomes pure information that is pure noise – and as all her inherited prejudices fall away, she 'is driven to discovery, to truth.'[9] Her 'objective is the creation of meaning between the imported information and the chaos that surrounds her.'[10] Meanwhile, the presence of the expelled in her new surroundings 'spontaneously causes an industrious creative activity in the vicinity of the expelled': in her alterity, she is 'a catalyst for the synthesis of new information.'[11] When these two creative pursuits 'are harmonized with each other, they transform in a creative manner not only the world, but also the original natives and the expelled.'[12] The freedom available to the expelled then is 'the freedom to change oneself and others as well.'[13] So 'exile, no matter what form it takes, is a breeding ground for creative activity, for the new.'[14]

Of course, the creativity that Flusser speaks of is of a civic and existential kind. But I have often been told that the narrative of the beginnings of our exile sounds like a film plot: 'You're going to make a film about this, right?' And indeed the rest of the story of our arrival in the UK has the makings of a very watchable thriller: a covert drive across the border into Ukraine, tapped phone lines, a midnight phone call, a departure without goodbyes. I have always resisted contemplating this. I've felt that we were far from the protagonists in the real story that was unfolding at the same time. I focused, instead, on the radical mundanity of making this new home livable (I'll leave to one side speculation with regard to potential causality between these events and me pursuing a creative career path in general). So why make a film about it?

It all started with an image. By chance I came across a photograph of what looked like Red Square with a large pool in the middle of it: there was the St Basil's Cathedral, with its patterned domes – Moscow's Eiffel Tower – there was the History Museum with the many towers of its roof glimmering silver like snow, there were the blue pine trees, the towers of the Kremlin,

Sasha Litvintseva, *Exile Exotic* (UK, 2015). Poolside of the Kremlin hotel, Antalya, Turkey.

From Exile to Entropy

the sun loungers, the parasols. This uncanny and unlikely combination of a place that pictorially signifies Russia but is physically inaccessible to us, via the apparatus of tourism and leisure, triggered in me an unravelling and a gathering that led eventually to our pilgrimage there. Yet along with our personal history, and the official history of the recent years that it is embedded in, and a product of, understanding the full ramifications of this image requires a deeper historical framing. We need to go back to go forward: through a single image our story becomes necessarily embedded in a process spanning centuries.

In 1555, half a century after Europe's great foray into the New World, the construction of St Basil's Cathedral began on the orders of Ivan the Terrible. This was to commemorate a major military victory – the taking of the city of Kazan – which cemented the end of the Golden Horde and the Tatar-Mongol yoke that had held dominion over Rus for centuries – this had profoundly and irreparably stalled its political and economic development causing it to fall behind the rest of Europe while intensifying the feudal exploitation of the Russian people. This was to remain so until the mid-nineteenth century. Then, within two generations of feudalism's abolition, the country sped into communism. Legend has it that Ivan the Terrible was so taken by the beauty of the cathedral that he ordered the architect's eyes to be taken out so as to make sure a more beautiful building was never built. And yet here we find ourselves gazing at its exact copy. The images I film of this replica become another layer of replication yet. The film *Exile Exotic* (2015) is permeated by doubles: the Kremlin Palace hotel in Antalya, Turkey is a double of the Kremlin, our pilgrimage a double pilgrimage – to the inaccessible motherland as well as to the touristic circumstances of its departure. And this doubled cathedral by the side of a pool is itself not without precedent.

The Cathedral of Christ the Saviour in Moscow took more than forty years to build and was destined to stand for as many. Erected in celebration of another military victory – the victory over Napoleon, a victory won by retreating and leaving nothing behind – it rose high above a city almost completely devastated by fire, set ablaze by its own citizens in anticipation of Napoleon's arrival. The city was never quite rebuilt until the capital was moved back there after the revolution by the Boksheviks – a symbolic gesture among others, such as the adoption of the Gregorian calendar and an unsuccessful experiment with a five-day week during the time of the Five Year Plan – who proceeded to blow up the cathedral in the 1930s, looking to replace religion with ideology in the people's superstitious hearts. The destroyed Cathedral of Christ the Saviour was to be replaced by the Palace of the Soviets, which would have been the tallest building in the world – dwarfing all of America's Babylonian ambitions – and a symbol of the victory of socialism, of a new country, a new Moscow. But this project never came to fruition, stalled by war as all other much-needed construction. The enormous foundations for it had been, however, already dug out before the war, and though the rest of the construction was abandoned, in the 1950s the crater for the foundations was filled with water and turned into an open-air swimming pool, 'Moskva.' Instead of religion, ideology; instead of a cathedral, a pool with a view of the Kremlin.

Millions of people fled Russia after the 1917 revolution; some left pre-emptively, others escaped, and many were expelled during the 1920s and 1930s. Intellectuals, businessmen, landowners, officers, as well as members of other factions of the revolutionary left – in their exiles across the globe, from Paris to Peru – believed their mission was to preserve the 'true' Russian culture and Orthodox Christianity until the end of what they saw as the Soviet occupation. Many of their symbols

From Exile to Entropy

were reinstated as Russian state symbols in the 1990s, including the tricolour and the Byzantine eagle. Meanwhile, the population that remained in Russia lived behind the Iron Curtain, forbidden from travelling and otherwise cut off from the rest of the so-called Free World, tasked with fostering a new national identity and putting into practice an untested political theory. Emigration was seen as treason, a punishable criminal offense. Much of it happened as defections, such as when ballet dancers and Olympic athletes fled their flights home, or when an oceanographer jumped overboard and swam ninety kilometres for days straight, without food or water, to the Philippine shore.

In the 1990s the ideological hole at the heart of new Russia was in turn plugged with a revival of Orthodox Christianity. Alongside many others my parents were baptised as adults. As a symbolic gesture the Cathedral of Christ the Saviour was rebuilt in the same place, exactly as it had been, as if the Soviet period had never happened – an act of revival that was as much a violent act of erasure as its destruction had been. Meanwhile, just when the pool with the view of the Kremlin disappeared, the borders were opened, international tourism became possible, and all who could afford it rushed abroad to make up for the lost time. The film begins as we find ourselves by the side of a pool with a view of the Kremlin. The tourists we are surrounded by are mostly Russian. My mother and I discuss what it might be that brings them here, given their options; we recall the pools we have been near since we were first able to travel, and all the ones we sat by when we had to leave Russia for good. We discuss the fate of the blown up cathedral, and even though my mother had visited the pool many times, she thinks I am making up the story about the plans for the Palace of the Soviets – failed plans were not broadcast. Revival and erasure go hand in hand with remembering and forgetting.

The scene by the pool is interrupted by found footage of

Sasha Litvintseva, *Exile Exotic* (UK, 2015). Underwater on the Red Square replica.

a military parade traversing the same ground at Red Square. The typical presumption by Western viewers is that this is archival footage from Soviet times, while in fact it is from the Victory Day parade of 2015, the year I made the film. Every year, on the 9th of May, the army marches through Red Square, not as a cyclical celebration of the past, but as a projection of future strength. This scene is overlaid with an operatic piece of music for voice, Theremin and loop pedal, in which layers of repetition weave a sonic ecology where singularity and multiplicity, the human and the non-human, become indistinguishable. The coordinated group performativity of the parade is echoed in the very last scene of the film, of a water aerobics class taking place in front of St Basil's Cathedral. The camera breaks the surface of the water, alternatively focusing on submerged bodies and their architectural surroundings. It's the last of the film's undulating waves of return and repetition, erasure and rebuilding, remembering and forgetting, a set of tides in wherein each element is followed by its opposite, which turns out to be its double. History seems to have not so much ended as short-circuited.

In 1986 a safety test at Chernobyl Nuclear Power Plant led to a reactor meltdown and a subsequent open-air graphite fire that raged for nine days, carrying radioactive fission products into the atmosphere and later leading to their precipitation over most of Europe. In the midst of the Cold War, the event that has become known as the Chernobyl nuclear disaster was a reminder of the power of the nuclear to obliterate history in the most straightforwardly apocalyptic sense. My father was meant to be at Chernobyl for the tests but by chance got held up at the Kola plant up north, covering for a colleague who was getting married. Had he gone, he would not have come back, I would not have been conceived and, so, would not be writing this now. My personal brush with this global nuclear disaster was in fact a missed connection: it is by my non-involvement that I exist. I am not a protagonist in this story – not even an extra – and yet (I can't help thinking) my entire existence rests upon my non-relation to this event.

In the 1990s it became legal to watch Hollywood films in Russia. As we indulged in apocalyptic blockbusters from the position of the historical rupture we were living in, the proposition of rapid, all-encompassing and irreversible change seemed more than speculative. A burgeoning genre in anticipation of the new millennium, these Hollywood fiction films are by necessity always scripted around a protagonist – think Liv Tyler's heartache as the entire world awaits destruction in *Armageddon*. My interest lies with the extras, cast en masse to appear in the action-filled scenes of their destruction. I pause the films on the close-ups of the extras' faces, in just a handful of frames emoting the fear of their own deaths at the end of the world. My film *Immortality, Home and Elsewhere* (2014) sets out from such an intersection of the incommensurability of a single life with the flux of historical events, and the incommensurability of history with deep time.

The naming of the Anthropocene, a recently proposed geological epoch in which humans are said to have made changes to the geophysical make-up of the Earth, has triggered discussion among scholars from a range of disciplines about the totalising nature of the name: who is the *anthropos* that is to blame? Indeed those responsible and those already feeling the effects of the ecological crisis are not evenly spread across the globe, and suggestions for a more appropriate designation include Capitalocene and Plantationocene.[15] The name has also triggered criticism for its hubristic portrayal of humans as able to wield power over the geological in its entirety, or able to prevent or even witness an event such as the end of the world.

Jeffrey Jerome Cohen writes that 'we crave apocalypse' because it reconfirms humanity as the pinnacle of historical and biological evolution: 'we have always lived in end times because climaxes that happen for us reassure that we are protagonists rather than actors in a non-anthropocentric tale.'[16]

In her contribution to *Twilight of the Anthropocene Idols*, Claire Colebrook sees the dominant narrative around the Anthropocene to be a final unification of humans as a species by the very threat of annihilation. This annihilation, having proven humankind's existence, must now be avoided at all costs: 'man exists, and must be saved.'[17] The 'we' as defined by the *anthropos* in the term 'Anthropocene' is the 'we' 'that is constituted precisely by way of a death sentence: I mourn my future non-being and therefore I am, and therefore survival is constituted as an imperative.'[18] Although, just as that which is 'human' is united under the threat and the guilt of the Anthropocene, it is immediately divided into perpetrator and victim, whereby a 'bad' humanity of excess has nearly destroyed the earth, and a 'good' eco-friendly humanity must survive and inherit it.[19] Hollywood blockbusters testify to her reading of the dominant cultural narrative; in fact, they contribute to its creation. From *Avatar* (2009) and *Interstellar* (2014) to *Mad Max: Fury Road* (2015), some of the biggest films in recent years have portrayed 'a destructive humanity [that] becomes the catalyst for human triumph, with a proper humanity emerging with sublimity from near death.'[20] The perpetuity of this depiction of humans as ultimately triumphant, together with the business-as-usual cinematography, editing and story arc, foreclose the possibility of contemplating the end of humankind, and thus make it possible to avoid responsibility for the Anthropocene or taking political action: no action is necessary when the future is guaranteed for the protagonists.

How to undo this insidious influence on the imaginary

From Exile to Entropy

wrought by narrative film? How to think futurity and collectivity through practice in the present, rather than assuredness of individual presence after the end of the world? I think to my father's absence from Chernobyl and our current presence after the supposed end of history. I think to the faces of the anonymous extras at the moment of their fictional death, standing in, collectively, individually, for the fictional death of a fictional humanity as a whole. I slow down these images and they form the beginnings of the visual make-up of the film. As Fredric Jameson attributes to a 'someone,' in a curious gesture of generosity toward collective anonymity, 'it is easier to imagine the end of the world than to imagine the end of capitalism.'[21] Why is it easier to imagine the end of the world as imminent than it is to imagine how to mark nuclear waste burial sites to communicate their danger into the future? Uranium, with its half-life as long as the Earth (this is, in fact, how the age of the Earth is determined), produces isotopes whose half-life is such that they will linearly propel themselves into deep time for hundreds of thousands of years. This is a certainty. Why then, even now that it has become a practical necessity, is it impossible to contemplate this certainty, and to imagine a humanity so far in the future, much less a semiotic code that would persist long enough? And conversely, why, in narrative terms, would the presence of sentient humans be necessary at the end of the world?

Five billion years from now our sun will be running out of hydrogen and beginning to die. As it dies it will expand and swallow up the planets one by one: such is the certain end of our world as a whole. The narrator of my film wonders – in the spirit of the pathos and confusion of scale implicit in the act of imagining oneself present at the end of the world – what will flash before her eyes as the sun dies five billion years from now.

Similarly, even if with different motives, Jean-François Lyotard considers the fate of thought on the deep-time scale of the eventual demise of the sun.[22] For him, time, in contrast to history, is the time on the scale of the cosmic, where humans are not the only possessors of minds that are capable of computation, memorisation and thought. His concern is how the ability for thought – that is, computation and memorisation – can go on after the solar explosion and, thus, to escape our bodies and the conditions of life on earth. My concern lies in analysing the origins of the desire to propel subjectivity into deep time.

In the spirit of tracing the intricacies of the incommensurability of subjectivity and deep time, one of the structural elements of *Immortality, Home and Elsewhere* is a text collage of two incommensurate scientific disciplines: astrophysics and neuropsychology. Taking from the latter the premise that subjective time is based on the overall information-processing rate, the text speculates on its implications against the two theories of the death of the universe. The open cosmology theory famously states that the universe will infinitely continue to expand. As a result, the temperature of the universe will approach absolute zero. With this, the sentients will experience a dramatic decrease in their information processing rates: time – subjective time, that is – will pass so rapidly that a year will seem like minutes. If subjective time is based on the overall information processing rate, then subjective experience of life's duration is based on the total information processed; consequently, life's duration can be measured in terms of the total information processed. At the heat death of the universe, the sentients will experience their life to be very short. The closed cosmology theory, on the other hand, states that the universe will not infinitely continue to expand, but rather that the present expansion of the universe will reverse so that the universe will eventually collapse. As a result, the temperature of the

From Exile to Entropy

universe will approach infinity. As the universe collapses and its temperature approaches infinity, the sentients will experience a dramatic increase in their information processing rates and, consequently, in their subjective time. Approaching this infinity, the sentients will experience their subjective time to be infinitely long: the sentients will therefore experience immortality as the universe ends.

> Don't want to close my eyes,
> I don't want to fall asleep,
> 'Cause I'd miss you, babe,
> And I don't want to miss a thing.

But let me bring this back down to Earth for a minute. As far-fetched as this cocktail of two different scales of abstraction is, the real incommensurability is between them and the situated and material now, such as it is. I heed Donna Haraway's call to account for where we are and where we are not.[23] The film begins with images of the house I live in, its interior and its immediate vicinity. In 'Taking Up Residence in Homelessness,' Flusser writes about the home in which he finally settled:

> I built myself a house in Robion, so that I could live there. My usual writing desk stands in the middle of the house with the usual disorder of books and papers. I have gotten used to the village surrounding my house. There is the usual post office and the usual weather. Things become more and more unusual the further I get away: Provence, France, Europe, the earth, the ever-expanding universe. Also, the past year, the lost homelands, the adventurous abysses of history and prehistory, the coming adventurous future, and the unforeseeable future behind it.[24]

My house in south London, built in the 1990s, was originally part of a council estate, one of a number of developments built on space left empty since the WWII bombings. All the estates in the area have decorative architectural features that have not aged very well in the last twenty years, but that also render them tragicomedically futuristic, science-fictional even. I walk beside them every day. As the film begins, the speculative text is delivered over images of these buildings. Situating yourself in the familiar is the first step in attempting to situate yourself amongst the unfolding scales of the inconceivable. And conversely, a desire to conceive of yourself in abstract time and space is not unrelated to the alienation wrought by the violence of history and place.

In another essay, aptly named 'On the End of History,' Flusser discusses the premise of the end of history from the point of view of the end of natural history; that is, the end of all process – the end of the universe. If history is necessarily a story and a story is necessarily historicising, then he puts forward the law of thermodynamics as the story that tells the entirety of natural history, beginning to inevitable end. However, he also argues that natural history and the natural sciences that narrate it, exist in a circular causality, resulting in a posthistorical condition. He uses a metaphor of film production and criticism to think through this:

The algorithm that formulates the second law of thermodynamics is an idea for a film. The German translation for this algorithm is the screenplay. The story of natural history is the film itself. The natural sciences are film criticism. What do they critique? The film? The screenplay? The film idea? The idea (the algorithm) comes from film criticism itself, from the natural sciences, which is to say, from thermodynamics. However, thermodynamics believes that the algorithm has been taken from the film. Someone has an idea. The idea is derived from a film that he will shoot. People can no longer be persuaded of this. Posthistory.[25]

He describes 'the vertigo,' the 'whirlwind,' 'the dizziness' – similarly to how he had described the dizziness of the groundlessness of exile – which accompanies the struggle of our nervous system to contemplate this schema of cause and effect, knowledge and story, entropy and time.[26] And he argues that this very dizziness

> Is the screw by means of which we unscrew ourselves from historical consciousness, to drill ourselves into another hole. The turns of the screw are processes, and our thought must move along these turns. Yet, the screw itself is not a process, but rather a form. Thus, we proceed from the process to the form, from the historical into the formal.[27]

When dealing with the intersections of nature and science, and the universe and the nervous system – the confusion over which predates, narrates, nestles, and which follows, is narrated, is nestled – is itself 'nothing more than a turning of the screw out of history and into posthistory,' as these things are only incommensurable and only make 'one dizzy when one thinks about this historically, but not when one thinks about it formally.'[28] How then to conceive of process as form, of time as not periodised but simultaneous, of space and time as differences of degree rather than kind? How to make this manifest?

Where we are and where we are not, where we are and where we are not able to be, spatially or temporally. An exile cannot return home, a sentient being is not able to be present at the heat death of the universe. I am not able to visit Chernobyl before the catastrophe; I am in theory able to visit its environs now, following existing paths of disaster tourism, but I am not

Sasha Litvintseva, *Immortality, Home and Elsewhere* (UK, 2014).
Google Street View walkthrough of the Giza plateau.

inclined to. My mother is not able to visit Red Square itself, but is able to visit its copy, as well as the real Eiffel Tower and the real Pyramids of Giza. The Pyramids are where she went on her very first trip out of Russia when she was first able to travel abroad in the 1990s. While I am making the film *Immortality, Home and Elsewhere*, Google releases Streetview walkthroughs of the Giza plateau, as well as of the Taj Mahal and the viewing platform atop the Eiffel Tower. The virtuality implicit in tourism is taken to its logical conclusion.

What is the value of being somewhere as opposed to not being there, of presence over absence, proximity over distance? What is the value of an experience and what counts as one? If the subjective experience of life's duration is based on the total information processed, would you risk groundlessness for the promise of being able to be everywhere at once? Flusser referred to the groundlessness of the condition of 'exile [as] an ocean of chaotic information,' and in the film, as the narrator asks what will flash before her eyes as the Earth gets consumed by the dying sun, we are virtually present on the streets of Moscow.²⁹ The interactive virtuality of Streetview is on par with the imagistic virtuality of cinema or the physical virtuality of a Kremlin replica. Yet mediated through cinema, Streetview carries the same indexical value as the mediated real thing, being one step removed from the physical world, and as such perhaps coming closer to accessing the inaccessible than the doubly mediated images of the replica Kremlin. Mediated through cinema, Streetview provides an entry point to experiencing the coexistences and simultaneities of spaces and times that define the physical world itself. And in the virtual presence it provides us, it designates our necessary absence: our theoretical ability to be present anywhere, but at home nowhere.

The temporality of these images is such that, as Robert Smithson writes, 'time does not pass during the actual moments of these intervals,' but rather it is a 'time [that] is solidified' and 'becomes an actual object.'³⁰ Through these images we are able to inhabit a point in space-time for indefinite durations, or travel from one point in space-time to another in no time at all. In 'Line and Surface,' Flusser draws on the difference between line/writing and surface/image to articulate his version of a posthistorical future, the potential for which he locates in the moving image. For him thinking in the form of linear writing represents 'the world by projecting it as a series of successions.'³¹ This has defined Western thought – which is to say historical thought – for the past thousand years, yet it is something that has started to change as visual media become increasingly prevalent. Flusser conceptualises the difference between the two as being primarily temporal:

> We must follow the written text if we want to get at its
> message, but in pictures we may get the message first, and

then try to decompose it. And this points to the difference between the one-dimensional line and the two-dimensional surface: the one aims at getting somewhere; the other is there already, but may reveal how it got there. This difference is one of temporality, and it involves the present, the past, and the future.[32]

An image presents its message to us immediately, but it acquires detail and depth with time: it offers a non-linear encounter, compared to the historical time of the text. The convergence of linear and surface thinking in moving images has the potential to 'impose a radically new structure on thought,' which 'implies a posthistorical being-in-the-world.'[33] Flusser proposes that a further fusion of line-surface thought in moving image could also 'enable us to think about facts that are presently unthinkable,' thus 'permitting us to rediscover a sense of "reality" and opening up "fields for a new type of thinking".'[34] Unlike the historical position in which 'processes are the method by which things become,' this new position of linear-surface fusion 'stands in that sort of time wherein processes are seen as forms.'[35] For Flusser, this non-linear, non-historical, temporal-visual language was an object of anticipation. I would like to propose that at the historical juncture we find ourselves, and with the emerging tools for mediating the moving image, this line-surface posthistorical condition is beginning to take shape.

Flusser refers to writing/line as one-dimensional and image/surface as two-dimensional. With the emergence of the line-surface posthistorical kind of filmmaking, we can begin to think of moving image as three-dimensional: a sedimentation of two-dimensional surfaces upon one another to form the depth of a three-dimensional temporal solid. What this creates is not the linear one-dimensional temporality of history, but rather a thick temporal object in which matter and time are

From Exile to Entropy

entangled, and a multitude of points in space-time coexist. Processes and artefacts, images and flows, bodies and architectures, all coexist in this solid temporal object that can be traversed in every direction: forward and backward into the past and future on the horizontal plane; or, up and down the vertical plane of deepening individual moments, the way Maya Deren sees verticality as a probing of 'the ramifications of the moment,' and as 'concerned with its qualities and its depth.'[36] Perhaps we ought to be thinking not so much of deep time and our fate therein, but of the deep now; that is, considering all environmental, human, historical, and material factors that make the current moment possible, from the magnetosphere, the spin of the earth, and the light of the sun, to the choices you, the real protagonist of this story, have made to be reading this now.

Notes

1   Francis Fukuyama, 'The End of History?', *The National Interest* 16 (Summer 1989): 3–18.

2   Bruno Latour, *We Have Never Been Modern* (Cambridge, MA: Harvard University Press, 1993).

3   Ibid., 8.

4   Robert Smithson, *Robert Smithson: The Collected Writings*, ed. Jack Flam (Berkeley: University of California Press, 1996), 105.

5   Sean Cubitt, *Finite Media: Environmental Implications of Digital Technologies*, (Durham: Duke University Press, 2017), 6.

6   Donna J. Haraway, 'Situated Knowledges: The Science Question in Feminism and the Privilege of Partial Perspective,' *Feminist Studies* 14, No. 3. (Autumn 1988): 575–99.

7   Vilém Flusser, *The Freedom of the Migrant: Objections to Nationalism,* trans. Kenneth Kronenberg (Urbana: University of Illinois Press, 2003), 3.

8   Vilém Flusser, 'Exile and Creativity,' in *Writings*, ed. Andreas Strohl, trans. Erik Eisel (Minneapolis: University of Minnesota Press, 2002), 104.

9   Ibid., 106.

10 Ibid., 108.

11 Ibid., 108.

12 Ibid., 108.

13 Ibid., 108.

14 Ibid., 109.

15 Donna J. Haraway, *Staying with the Trouble: Making Kin in the Chthulucene* (Durham: Duke University Press, 2016).

16 Jeffrey Jerome Cohen, *Stone: An Ecology of the Inhuman* (Minneapolis: University of Minnesota Press, 2015), 85.

17 Tom Cohen, Claire Colebrook and J. Hillis Miller, *Twilight of the Anthropocene Idols* (London: Open Humanities Press, 2016), 88.

18 Ibid., 82.

19 Ibid., 83.

20 Ibid., 85.

21 Fredric Jameson, *Archaeologies of the Future: The Desire Called Utopia and Other*

Science Fictions (Durham: Duke University Press, 2005), 199.

22 Jean-François Lyotard, *The Inhuman: Reflections on Time* (Stanford: Stanford University Press, 1991).

23 Haraway, 'Situated Knowledges: The Science Question in Feminism and the Privelege of Partial Perspective.'

24 Flusser, 'Taking Up Residence in Homelessness,' *Writings*, 100.

25 Flusser, 'On the End of History,' 145–6.

26 Ibid., 146.

27 Ibid., 146.

28 Ibid., 148.

29 Flusser, 'Exile and Creativity,' *Writings*, 104.

30 Smithson, *Robert Smithson: The Collected Writings*, 32.

31 Flusser, 'Line and Surface,' *Writings*, 21.

32 Ibid., 23

33 Ibid., 26.

34 Ibid., 31.

35 Ibid., 33.

36 Maya Deren, 'Poetry and the Film: A Symposium' (1953), transcribed on ubuweb, accessed April 12, 2017, www.ubu.com/papers/poetry_film_symposium.html.

References

Cohen, Jeffrey Jerome. *Stone: An Ecology of the Inhuman.* Minneapolis: University of Minnesota Press, 2015.

Cubitt, Sean. *Finite Media: Environmental Implications of Digital Technologies.* Durham: Duke University Press, 2017.

Deren, Maya. 'Poetry and the Film: A Symposium.' Originally took place 1953. Transcribed on ubuweb. Accessed 12 April 2017. http://www.ubu.com/papers/poetry_film_symposium.html

Flusser, Vilém. *Writings*. Ed. Andreas Strohl, trans. Erik Eisel. Minneapolis: University of Minnesota Press, 2002.

Fukuyama. Francis. 'The End of History?'. *The National Interest* 16, Summer 1989: 3–18.

Haraway, Donna J. 'Situated Knowledges: The Science Question in Feminism and the Privilege of Partial Perspective.' *Feminist Studies* 14, No. 3. Autumn 1988.

Haraway, Donna J. *Staying with the Trouble: Making Kin in the Chthulucene.* Durham: Duke University Press, 2016.

Jameson, Fredric. *Archaeologies of the Future: The Desire Called Utopia and Other Science Fictions.* Durham: Duke University Press, 2005.

Latour, Bruno. *We Have Never Been Modern.* Cambridge, MA: Harvard University Press, 1993.

Lyotard, Jean-François. *The Inhuman: Reflections on time.* Stanford: Stanford University Press, 1991.

Smithson, Robert. *Robert Smithson: The Collected Writings*. Edited by Jack Flam. Berkeley: University of California Press, 1996.

From Exile to Entropy

2
Endotic Investigations

Domestic Tourism II:
Scene Typology

Maha Maamoun

Thumbnail	Title	Scene Genre
	Farhan Mulazim Adam Director: Umar Abdel-Aziz	Romance / Nationalism
	The Night Baghdad Fell Director: Mohammad Amin	Espionage / Nationalism
	Excuse Us, We are Seeing Rough Times Director: Sherif Mandour	Gender Politics

A look
through a collection of scenes from
Egyptian feature films
that have been filmed against the backdrop of
the Pyramids
shows different ways in which these
icons of the past
are re-appropriated from the
timelessness of the touristic postcard
and re-inscribed into the complex and dynamic narratives of the city.

Scene Typology from the multi-disciplinary project *Domestic Tourism* by Maha Maamoun.

Description	Ruling Sentiment	Year
He wonders about Egyptians' disinterest in their glorious ancient heritage. She changes the subject to talk about her father in prison, whom he should meet.	Frustrated Patriotism and Dysfunctional Relationship	2005
Two American spies, on a mission to Egypt to find a young man developing Weapons of Mass Defense, confirm their determination to find him and to end the threat he poses to American national security.	American Megalomania	2005
Local male tourist guide gives female Western tourist advice to dress conservatively to keep her fiance's interest alive.	Wisdom and Universality of Local Knowledge	2005

Thumbnail	Title	Scene Genre
	What a Loss Director: Ali Abdel-Khalek	Past Glory vs. Present Corruption
	A Mood of Love Director: Saad Hindawi	Worth of Nations
	A Woman and Five Men Director: Alaa Karim	Beauty of Egypt
	al-Hilali's Fist Director: Ibrahim Afifi	Fight Against Powers of Evil
	Playing with Big Shots Director: Sherif Arafa	Past Glory vs. Present Corruption
	The Death Squad Director: Atef al-Tayeb	Fight Against Powers of Evil

Description	Ruling Sentiment	Year
Wife of undertaker implores her husband to not give up on Egypt, and to continue his fight against the corruption of government officials who continue to block his project.	Determination vs. Desperation	2003
Friends discuss the comparative merits of Egyptians vs. the French. The French 'take everything they do seriously'. But 'Egyptians are kind-hearted'. But then she questions the value of kindness ...	Self-doubt + Glorification or Demonization of the Other	2004
He tells her that he has traveled the world but found 'no place more beautiful than Egypt, and especially the Pyramids'. They climb the Pyramid, and he proposes to her at the top.	Machismo	1997
Shaken by a vision he had at the Pyramids, where a voice calls on him to stand on the side of Truth, Light and Wisdom, al-Hilali finally rises up to the challenge, and decides to pursue his assailants.	Truth and Good Shall Prevail	1991
A telephone operator and his friend decide to continue their difficult fight against a corrupt system. But their enemies are in high places.	Determination vs. Desperation	1990
He is still trying to clear his name from a crime that tainted his integrity and national loyalty at a time of war. But his enemy is unknown. 'It could be Fate or a country whose army had besieged Suez ... '	Desperation	1989

Thumbnail	Title	Scene Genre
	The Tiger and the Female Director: Samir Seif	Fight Against Powers of Evil
	Love by the Pyramids Director: Atef al-Tayeb	Romance / Difficult Present
	The Queen's Honey Director: Husam al-Din Mustafa	Fight for Power
	The Bus Driver Director: Atef al-Tayeb	Past Glory vs. Present Corruption
	Case Unsolved Director: Medhat al-Sibai	Past Glory vs. Present Corruption
	Ascending to the Abyss Director: Kamal al-Sheikh	Espionage / Nationalism

Description	Ruling Sentiment	Year
Senior police officer chides one of his officers for screwing up and failing to interrupt a major drug deal.	Determination vs. Desperation	1987
Ali and Ragaa seek refuge at the Pyramids from the noise and aggression of the city, only to be arrested by the Police for their public display of affection.	Dreams for the Future Crushed by Cruel Present	1986
The two strong men of the town fight over the town's leadership. The winner of the fight shall be obeyed by all.	Machismo + Greed for Power	1985
In a time of wrenching socio-economic changes, ex-comrades meet to lament about the good old days – days of solidarity, sacrifice and love.	Lamentation	1983
Jinxed junior security guard is given a last chance and assigned to guard the Pyramids. The Pyramid of Cheops goes missing on his watch. Nationwide investigations follow.	Defenselessness	1981
Egyptian intelligence officer on a plane back to Egypt asks the captured Egyptian spy to look out the window as they fly over the Pyramids. 'The Pyramids ... The Nile. This is Egypt', he says.	Patriotism vs. Shame	1978

Thumbnail	Title	Scene Genre
	The M Empire Director: Hussein Kamal	Romance/ Difficult Present
	Eve on the Way Director: Hussein Helmy al-Mohandis	Romance/ Feminism
	The Bride of the Nile Director: Fateen Abdel-Wahab	Glorious Past/ Glorious Present
	No Time for Love Director: Salah Abu Sei	Nationalism/ Struggle for Independence
	A Love Story Director: Helmy Halim	Romance
	Ismail Yassin on a Trip to the Moon Director: Hamada Abdel-Wahab	Soft Sci-fi

Description	Ruling Sentiment	Year
Single mother-of-six meets her patient lover who insists on waiting for her till she's ready. She tells him of her children's rebelliousness and latest decision to run elections at home.	Love + Confusion vis-a-vis Profound Changes of the Social Order and Hierarchies of Power	1972
Staunch Feminist decides to throw herself from the top of the Pyramid out of desperation and as a PR act to help her cause.	Fight for Women's Rights + Female Frailty	1968
He tells her the Pyramids are a sign of the old days' tyranny and injustice. She, a visitor from the ancient past, defends the justice of the Past and explains that they were built to give people jobs.	Optimism of a Socialist Present vs. Belief in a Glorious Past	1963
On a school trip to the Pyramids, the teacher meets and falls in love with one of the members of a clandestine movement fighting against the British occupation and their local allies.	National Pride + Belief in the Future	1963
She knows he is dying young of an unknown disease. He insists on talking about their future life together. She wants to record their convertation so that she can listen to it later.	Love + (In)Finiteness of Time	1959
On its way back from a trip to the moon, the rocket flies over the Pyramid, carrying in it a scientifically advanced human race who had long taken refuge in the moon after the nuclear war.	Belief in the Present	1959

Mapping Urban Space and Time, Talking to Horses and Pigs

Edwina Attlee

There They Carved A Space is a performed essay, using voice, film and sound on stage, by Claire Healy and Emilia Weber. Created between 2014 and 2015, the piece comprises original and archival film footage, an original soundscape by Anneke Kampman and a spoken text collaged from existing and original texts. The performance opens with the two authors on stage; they begin to speak as film is projected onto them. They address the politics of space; in particular, concepts of the commons and the commoner in the context of land value, the housing market, home ownership and homelessness in the United Kingdom. A long history is cited, including the Enclosures Act of 1801 and the redevelopment of the area surrounding the Lea Valley ahead of the 2012 Olympics. There is emphasis on the ideology and building plans of the Welfare State, and the demolition, redevelopment and sale of many of these estates and institutions. Healy and Weber propose a series of traits belonging to 'the commoner': 'reciprocity, willingness to argue, long memory, collective celebration.'[1] The essay takes its shape firstly from this history, anachronistic though it is; and secondly from the structuring device of a series of visits, made by the speakers, to the places they have lived. It therefore moves around in space and time, and is characterised by the collision of the apparently personal – memories of sickness, childhood, descriptions of family photographs and homes – and the more explicitly political – demonstrations, evictions, footage from news reports, acts of parliament and local government.

Tom Phillips' mapping project *20 Sites, n Years* began in 1973. The *n* in its title signals Phillips' intention that it be unending, and he has made plans for it to continue after his death. Each year the artist visits twenty sites in Camberwell in south London. At each site he takes some photographs from, where possible, precisely the same position. The photographs are taken in order and at approximately the same time of day each year.[2] The shooting position is marked by a splodge of paint sprayed by the

Tom Phillips, *20 Sites, n Years*, work in progress, begun 1973, photographic prints. Site 11, *In the Housing Estate,* was visited and photographed by the artist at approximately 2.45pm each year. He remarks 'If *20 Sites* were a symphony (which of course it is) then sites 9 to 12 constitute its slow movement.'

artist onto the ground, fence, wall or tree. The project is an accumulation of images with brief captions. It is the map of a walk, made again and again. The images can be viewed online in a slide show on the artist's website. Phillips has called them 'twenty locations that describe a circle.'[3]

Jake Auerbach's 2016 film *20 Sites, n Years* allows audiences to see Phillips' project in progress. We meet the artist turning crackling pages of laminated typewriter paper at a table in his studio. The film follows him through the making and history of the artwork. His first words are, 'I think round about here is the start'. Like the artist, the film 'visits' each of the sites in turn, making a reading of each through a selective but chronological series of photographs. Phillips' voiceover tells us what to look for, and at times we are also shown 'the script,' a typewritten set of notes under the 'title' of whichever site we're currently examining. Auerbach's voiceover interjects only occasionally, to frame the artist ('a Renaissance man') and his relationship with the area ('Phillips does not just record the changes in his local area, he is also their author'). The sounds of the twenty sites are recorded and played as they are shown on screen, adding a dimension of movement to the static images.

Common change

There They Carved A Space opens on a black stage to the sound of a crackling recording of a female voice singing. Light comes in the form of the flicker of blank film, and the two performers begin to speak. Minutes later the film starts to play, engulfing them in its projection. As they mix up phrases, repeat part or whole of what has gone before, and throw their voice – quoting members of parliament, books, poems and the language of construction hoarding – it is clear that we hear many different voices.

They enter without announcement and it is more important that the audience recognise the text as an oral collage than that they know who is being referenced.

The film footage is like a wash: 'a thin coat of paint ... a broad thin layer of watercolour laid on freely with the brush ... a broad area of particular colour, light, shade.'[4] The two figures on stage almost disappear into it, whilst the images shown are almost always exterior shots, showing slow-moving or slowed-down motion. The imagery can be characterised as scenery rather than subject, the stage fills with long shots of ripples on the surface of lakes, wind through dappled leaves, fields of corn, swimming pools, scenes of construction and demolition, of traffic, estates in the sunshine; some show the sites described in the spoken text. The focus is blurred. Sometimes the spoken text corresponds with what is being shown, sometimes not. Below I cite the opening words of the piece – the two voices speak in turn and then at once.

Explicit in *There They Carved A Space* is doubt about what it means to look back, however far, in time. Their account of historical subversives – including the Whiteboys, the gleaners, the women of Greenham Common, and present-day squatters in the Aylesbury Estate – draws a through-line of urgency. These are figures Michel de Certeau would describe as tactical, making do with what they can get: they are cited as exemplary commoners.[5] Stitching the past into present concerns, creating a history and some sense out of 'a dissatisfaction with the present,' the piece performs 'a nostalgia conscious of itself.'[6] This self-consciousness is furthered by the way the text draws attention to its construction: 'we stop to film kennington park,' 'we stop to film the hoarding at st.agnes place', 'we drive in the fiat panda'. Stopping and looking, driving and recording, are presented as valid forms of research and dissent, and practical ways of measuring doubt. The way the text is repeated, and certain phrases become refrains, gives the sense of a doubtful set of voices; the essay becomes a space where ideas or arguments are being tested and tried out rather than simply declaimed.

E:
In spite of all the other
stairways.

C:
And you think about the light
and the air
with people + spaces

E:
Two boys one girl

the going was wet had to
scramble often

C:
suffering under a glass roof

once a small fishing village

1993 sockless on the balcony

once a small fishing village

our first home is physically
inscribed in us

a group of organic habits

we recapture the reflexes
of the first

two boys, one girl
young parents.

1993 sockless on the balcony

andrea brady writes of the
automatic dissonance

I alter my speech – rephrase to
mask my latest intonation

na clocha liatha, greystones

In spite of all the other stairways

It is run by handsome, regularly
photographed twins[7]

Mundane instances of inner city architecture, familiar street scenes and vehicles, and equally familiar figures: children, adults, workmen and the occasional animal – the people and objects in the photographs that make up *20 Sites* are frustratingly mute, and seeing what's in them takes a lot of looking. In sequence, however, and with Phillips' suggestive narration in Auberbach's film, they are hugely enticing; they can be treated as documents, read as evidence, scanned for clues. If you read the images as a series of self-referential 'spot the differences' that compare 'now' to 'then,' you can criticise the project for cute, ineffectual nostalgia. While it is true that there is a certain melancholy to some of the sequences – particularly those that witness the disappearance of shops, shop types, pubs and other buildings – there is also an amusing stubbornness and lively animation to the series: they are surprising, they develop their own logics, they seem to play with their viewer.

Auerbach's *20 Sites* draws to a close with Phillips talking about 'the changefulness of change itself.' Taking the sites in isolation and in tandem in the film makes this changefulness clear; no two sites move at the same pace, some are sites of constant action and adjustment, others leap forward or stand still, while in others we see 'the return of the past.' Phillips engages with the question of nostalgia through his intention that the project be unending: 'There is no outcome, not I nor Leo [his son] nor his heirs will ever see a result.'[8] His stance is not so much dissatisfaction with the present as a simple admission that it will soon be past. The decision to hold no ground, to resist the satisfaction of 'results' is a tactical one:

> it would be legitimate to define the *power of knowledge* by this ability to transform the uncertainties of history into readable spaces ... the space of a tactic is the space of the other ... What it wins it cannot keep. This nowhere gives a tactic mobility to

be sure, but a mobility that must accept the chance offerings of the moment...[9]

Refusing an 'outcome,' the project maps without limiting, and retains its uncertainty.

The protagonists' homes are used in both projects, but the idea of home – the object or starting point of nostalgia proper – is not the subject of either. Phillips makes a study of the façade of his family home and its immediate surroundings, but the identical treatment of this personal site to all the others allows any difference in the way it is read to be decided upon by the viewer (if they care, or notice, or not). Healy and Weber's approach is more sentimental, and more lopsided in the special presence of their childhood homes. What could be cloying and emotionally heavy-handed is intriguing. It is a cliché to remark on the difference in affect of the detail and the statistic, but here the stray detail of what feels like biography is set alongside other details of observation that are clearly biographical of contemporary urban space – for example the refrain of 'bolt-on balconies.' This patchwork of details brings the childhood homes of the authors into a common present, and underlines the 'long memory' of the commoners they describe. Both projects rebuke the shortsightedness of those in positions of relative power, the people in charge of many of the changes recorded in Phillips' photographs. This is a shortsightedness that ignores the long memory of the commoner, as well as the anachronism of time. The specific nostalgia invoked in *There They Carved* suggests a way of countering such short sight. Likewise, Phillips offers an alternative image of timeliness.

Fieldwork

In 1974 Harold Orton and Nathalia Wright produced *A Word Geography of England*. The book comprises 251 word maps based on material from the *Survey of English Dialects*. The survey, made between 1950 and 1961, documented 'dialectical English as spoken by the older generation.'[10] As it had been established that agricultural communities best preserved vernacular speech it was the farmer and his household who were studied. The maps show areas of lexical distribution: regions characterised by the employment of an individual word. The expressions mapped relate to the topics that were surveyed, which were as follows: the farm, farming, animals, nature, the house and housekeeping, the human body, numbers, time and weather, social activities, states, actions,relations. In total, 313 communities were surveyed. Responses were transcribed using the phonetic alphabet by fieldworkers – tape recorders were available from 1952 but the survey could not afford one.

The maps depict an oddly ahistorical scene, looking as they do to document non-standard vocabulary tethered to particular use and location. They contain no 'new' words which might better anchor them to the linear history of politics ('welfare,' for example) or war ('ration'). The maps map oral culture. Maps 31–40 show the expressions used by farmers to call their animals. The question used to discover these was: 'How do you call your animals in from the field?' To horses you shout (depending on where you are):

Cop
Cup
Kep
Come along cup
Come along cup cup

Come on cup
Come on cup cup
Come on kep
Cop (to a gelding)
Cop cop
Cup come on
Cup cup
Cup cup come along
Cup cup come on
Cup cup cup come along
Co-hope
Coop
Cope
Cowp
Cop cope
Come coop

To pigs:

Chack
Check
Giss
Jack
Pig
Tig
Check check
Giss giss
Gissy
Hurry tig tig
Pig pig
Piggy
Tig tig
Tig tig tig
Took-tig

Chig

Chug

Chuck

Chig chig

Chigs chigs

Chucky

Chuggy

Chuggy chug chug[11]

It is delightful, and makes perfect sense, to discover that horses need to be spoken to differently than pigs. It is more delightful still to see how this call varies between regions – and how it doesn't. Similarly pleasurable frictions and discoveries can be found in the records of expressions that are not purely aural; for example, those elicited by the question 'What do you call the inner layer of fat round the kidneys of a pig?' The responses include: Apron, Flare, Flea, Fleed, Flick, Leaf, Saim, Laird-Saim, Leaf-Fat, Leaf-Grease, Leaf of Fat, Pig's Leaf.[12] The demands made on a reader by this repetition and difference are similar to those made by Phillips' series of images. The poet Caroline Bergvall's concept of 'tactical authorship'[13] and her versioning 'translations' in the long poem sequence *Drift* highlight the political dimension beyond pleasure of the documentation of linguistic variation.[14] In each instance the recording or writing of alternatives suggests a counter to official, singular accounts. In the case of the word maps, the variation of spoken English counters ideas of a singular or acceptable national speech.

The linguistic survey that led to the construction of the *Word Geography* involved fieldworkers meeting with people throughout England. These people (referred to as 'informants' by fieldworkers) were encouraged to talk with 'the utmost freedom' about things they knew or cared about, particularly

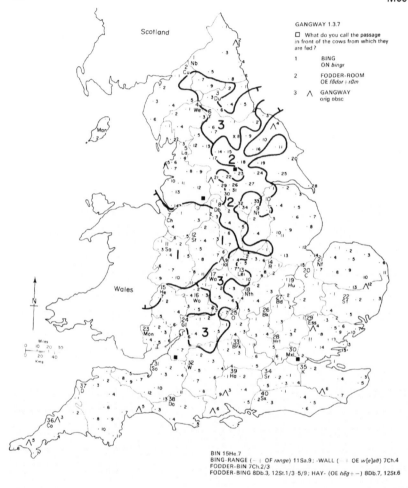

GANGWAY 1.3.7

☐ What do you call the passage
in front of the cows from which they
are fed?

1   BING
           ON *bingr*

2   FODDER-ROOM
           OE *fōdor* + *rūm*

3   ∧   GANGWAY
           orig obsc

BIN 15He.7
BING-RANGE (− + OF *range*) 11Sa.9; -WALL (− + OE *w[e]all*) 7Ch.4
FODDER-BIN 7Ch.2/3
FODDER-BING 8Db.3, 12St.1/3-5/9; HAY- (OE *hēg* + −) 8Db.7, 12St.6

Map 53 from the *Word Geography of England*, compiled by Harold Orton and Natalia Wright,
showing the geographic distribution of the words 'bing,' 'fodder-room' and 'gangway.'
The question that generated the map was 'what do you call the passage in front of the cows
from which they are fed?'

matters of local interest or the informant's occupation (commonly ploughing, hedging or stacking).[15] The fieldworker aimed to establish 'a friendly pupil-and-master relationship with his informant, who naturally played the role of master.' We can query how natural such role play was, as throughout this talk, the fieldworker would be taking notes by phonetic transcription, but an atmosphere of casual intimacy was important, as 'at all times … free, natural speech was the target. The primary instance was not the substance of what he said, but rather how he said it.'[16] This operation is at once dismissive and highly attentive to the person who speaks. The relationship between the interviewer and the informant (the 'pupil' and 'teacher') is one where a real and false ignorance are present at the same time.

What do you call the teeth at the back?

What was their word in the old days for separating the grain from the husks?

What is this I'm wearing? [*point at trousers*]

The 'utmost freedom' of the informant's speech is what Phillips is after from his subjects because he does not know what 'the answer' or indeed the subject will turn out to be. The asking of questions, and the active inclusion of evidence of this constructed fieldwork, is key to Phillips, as to Weber and Healy. Both projects call to attention the interactive nature of knowledge and meaning generated between fieldworker and respondent.[17]

Healy and Weber take this a step further and put themselves in the picture – making their bodies vulnerable to being looked at. They resist the 'flattening out' of the easily legible image, and the relative safety of 'critical distance.'[18] The script reads, 'to talk about a place is inevitably to abuse it in some way or another / so you place yourself in the picture / stop to film henry moore's reclining figure no. 3 / still nestled under the tower blocks.'[19] Here abuse is linked with distance; its counter is physical intimacy, the sharing of the same space. This is closely connected to de Certeau's assertion of the 'blindness' of the ordinary practitioners of the city, with his affection and respect for their 'blind knowledge,' as well as an assertion of the erotics of such positions: 'these practitioners make use of spaces that cannot be seen; their knowledge, of them is as blind as that of lovers in each other's arms.'[20] The poet Andrea Brady, cited in the script, describes her poetic collage practice as 'a bringing of the external world into the space of the personal in order to justify the attention to the personal.'[21] *There They Carved A Space* uses the two voices of its authors, and the many voices they cite, to create a sense of a shared 'personal.' The friction between different versions of the same idea, or different experiences of 'home,' reiterates their vision of difference-in-common.

Erasure

A final reading of the accumulating series of images that make up *20 Sites* is as a visual erasure. Phillips is known for his gargantuan erasure project on the Victorian novel *A Humument*, which he began in 1966. He first treated the novel with pen, gouache and watercolour, turning the book into an illuminated manuscript with a strange and unexpected narrative. The book has been through eight full 'treatments,' and has also spawned an opera and an app. It is through a reading of the poet Mary Ruefle's erasures that comparisons or family resemblances with *20 Sites* become clear.[22] Her definition of the practice is: 'the creation of a new text by disappearing the old text that surrounds it.'[23] Her erasure book, *A Little White Shadow*, reveals

Claire Healy and Emilia Weber stand amid text and fields on stage at the Rag Factory, performing *There They Carved A Space* (UK, 2016). The text offers a definition, in French and English, of the term 'gleaner.'

itself in the tension between inked type on yellowing paper (the pages of a book published 'for the benefit of a summer home for working girls' in 1889) and banks of white paint redacting what was underneath.[24] The effect is muted but suspenseful, the pages are mainly white, with each line of text distinct in structure even if it has been completely erased. Erasure feels like the wrong word; these lines have not been rubbed out but layered and piled with white – mattress on top of mattress as if to hide a pea. Often grains of a letter or phrase can be seen peeping through the white – Ruefle says she sometimes feels as though she is 'bandaging' the words, and that those that remain are the blood that 'seeped out.'[25] The violent tension, between an original text and one fashioned from or with it, is expressed in equally bloody terms by Antoine Compagnon when he writes about citation.

> When I cite, I excise, I extract. There is a primary object,
> placed before me, a text I have read, that I am reading,
> and the course of my reading is interrupted by a phrase.
> I return to the beginning; I reread. The phrase reread
> becomes a formula, isolated from the text. The rereading
> separates it from that which precedes and that which follows.
> The chosen fragment converts itself into a text no longer,
> a bit of text, a part of a sentence or a discourse, but a chosen
> bit, an amputated limb, not yet a transplant, but already
> an organ, cut off and placed in reserve.[26]

Citation and erasure seem to be two sides of a similar operation. Both can also be read as collage techniques in which alternative contexts are made to collide.[27] Throughout *A Little White Shadow*, tension is held between what remains and what is erased, partly through the time it takes for your eyes to travel across white banks of page to find the next word (the pages are mostly paint), and partly through an antagonism of sorts between the new text and the one it has been carved out of.

Andrea Brady describes the dissonance of time, place and memory, where, contrary to expectation it is knowing a place better that leads to a feeling of dislocation: 'There's an automatic dissonance between the memory of a place first seen and the same place when it's come to be familiar: they must be two different places. It's the same with the photographs, some so unlike who you are now, others hold your present face on a set of neat pins.'[28] The idea of a 'present face' is suggestive for a reading of Phillips' photographs particularly as his accumulating images offer faces that are continually slipping. Dissonance here can be understood as an unbidden consciousness of time; this is what gives the erasures their tension and what creates the internal logic of Phillips' sequences of photographs. The pinning of an image can also be thought about in terms of a cut or citation, 'an amputated limb ... cut off and placed in reserve.'[29] What is startling about Phillips' *20 Sites* is that his images, though leading very clearly to 'the creation of a new text by disappearing the old text that surrounds it,' have not been cut off so much as planted – the series gives the impression of growth.

Ruefle and Phillips practice a gradual and gentle destruction, where the presence of time is used, and held, in a grid, made of pages in a book, or images in a series of slideshows. The frame is key – Ruefle describes her erased books as containing poetry rather than poems: 'I do think of them as poetry, especially in sequence and taken as a whole.'[30] The shift from writing poems (which have beginnings and ends) to writing a new text of poetry, is significant and permits or encourages a more scattered reading. Scattered but not scattergun – there is a suggested structure to the reading; in 'Dew,' the pages are arranged in pairs, each half replies to or completes the one that comes before.

moonlight   sounded like

                                      murmured   the excited brain of

     long white fingers

                                         Browning

       as they came in contact with a

large tear

      forty years   on the platform   And   when the train pulled

                                    up

of a railway station

                                    he motioned with his hand to

                                   be left

     waited for a train   alone[31]

She says of poetry: 'the lines of a poem are speaking to each other, not you to them or they to you.'[32] This could be applied to the sequence of photographs that make up *20 Sites*, a warning perhaps to readers who want to impose heavy-handed meaning onto the ongoing chatter between image and image, but an invitation too, to read between and listen. The collagist and poet Joe Brainard writes,

> The material does it all. You have a figure and a flower and you add a cityscape and it makes the story. You have control if you want to take it but that's something I never wanted to do much. I mean if a story came out I'd sort of follow it, but I never want to read or make a story deliberately.[33]

This sense of a living material – which the poet, collagist or map maker just needs to follow, listen to, or *pick* – reiterates the collaborative sense of this kind of work and lets us think about this kind of writing or image-making as a form of flower arrangement.

> The only way I can describe it is like this: the words rise above the page – by say an eighth of an inch – and hover there in space, singly and unconnected, and they form a kind of field, and from this field I pick my words as if they were flowers.[81]

The metaphor of arranging flowers is significant for a collection of migratory images because it admits that the material under consideration is or was once *growing*. The unending promise of Phillips' project captures this sense of wild growth, his images (many of which depict the growth of both plant life and buildings) are paused and plucked – their arrangement reveals their untamed nature. The film footage in *There They Carved A Space* collages found footage, old news reports and snippets from documentaries, with film taken by the two speakers – 'up-to-date' images from the places described in the text. The anachronistic splicing makes time in the piece untidy and restless, mimicking the unhappy but un-forgetful experience of the commoner. In this flower arrangement the cut flowers decay at different speeds, and then sit out of synch in the same jug.

Ruefle is being characteristically playful when she talks about the beginnings and ends of erasure. Part of the fascination for her is that the material for future erasures is so copious, and that no single erasure can be the last – she says she hopes to be working on one when she dies. She describes the unexpected joy of finding a second copy of the same out-of-print book and realising that she could erase it again so that she wouldn't find the same words on a single page. The poet Anne Carson would suggest this joy responds to 'the benevolence of the untranslatable,' a glimpse of some third place 'between chaos and naming, between catastrophe and cliché.'[35] For Bergvall and de Certeau the untranslatable is related to the limited vision that requires tactical action – and yet, as both Phillips and Healy and Weber's work makes clear, this is a position of paradoxical sight.

Their arrangements inhabit the place 'between chaos and naming,' and in doing so discover, or make plain, that it can never be a destination or an 'ending.' To *end* would mark a step away from the tactical and into the strategic; it might mark the gaining of power, but it would be power that agrees with the existing frameworks and categories of power. One of the strange things about writing about Ruefle's erasures is that they resist transcription. You can type out the words she lets remain, but you cannot transcribe the layers of gouache, or the collision of yellowing paper with cold white-blue Tipp-ex and scrawly biro. The *20 Sites* images too are transliterations that resist transcription. There is a jumble of record and the un-recordable in both *20 Sites* and *There They Carved*, and pleasure lies in the friction between the two. Talking to horses and pigs is one thing, writing down the words you use is another. The oral historian William Schneider writes:

> Recording and writing about stories may fix their meaning
> in place, and without other recordings and context, meaning
> can get sandwiched and packaged in ways that distort
> meaning. The oral tradition is timeless; the written record
> seeks closure.[36]

Ruefle would put it like this: 'so sometimes we just stumble upon an act of erasure and recognise its beauty and seek to preserve it – seek to preserve that which has not been preserved; we make compositions out of decompositions.'[37] Better yet: cup cup cup, cohope, come along cup.

Notes

1 Claire Healy and Emilia Weber, *There They Carved A Space,* 2016 script, 5.

2 Tom Phillips, *20 Sites, n Years,* 2016, www.tomphillips.co.uk/works/20-sites-n-years.

3 Phillips, ibid.

4 *Shorter Oxford English Dictionary* (Oxford: O.U.P., 2007), 3,580.

5 'The Whiteboys in Ireland / who wore white smocks / met in the darkness of night to level the fields / to protest against rackrents, tithe collections, evictions / and the taking of the commonage by the land-owning elite', 'the gleaners / their practice is almost entirely in the control of women / they gather leftover stacks of grains after the main harvest / led by their own, the gleaner's queen', Healy and Weber, 6. Michel de Certeau, *The Practice of Everyday Life,* trans. Steven Rendall (London: University of California Press, 1988), 92–3.

6 Healy and Weber, *There They Carved A Space,* 5.

7 Ibid., 2.

8 Jake Auerbach dir., *20 Sites, n Years.*

9 de Certeau, 36–7.

10 Harold Orton, *A Word Geography of England* (New York: Souvenir, 1974), 1.

11 Ibid., 44–6, 136–7 (maps 3, 3A, 4, 4A, 5, 81, 81A).

12 Ibid., 50 (map 9).

13 'It has been happening to us, around us, slowly within us. Actions of pointing, of naming, of denouncing. That claim the enemy in our midst, not the enemy within. Don't let this be my finger. We have moved from the greedy liberalism of 'don't ask don't tell' to the authoritarian religiosity of the one and only.' Caroline Bergvall, 'Pressure Points', *How2 Journal,* 2007, www.asu.edu/piper/how2journal/vol_3_no_3/bergvall/pdfs/bergvall-pressure-points.pdf.

14 Caroline Bergvall, *Drift* (Callicoon: Nightboat Books, 2014).

15 Orton, *A Word Geography,* 1.

16 Ibid.

17 Olesen, Virginia L. and Elvi Whittaker, 'Role-making in participant observation: processes in the research – actor relationship,' *Human Organisation,* 26, 1967, 273–81.

18 'Using highly spatialized language, Armstrong argues that it is the feeling/thought binary which itself installs a form of critique where the subject is located in a position of power "over" the text as other, producing a form of distant rather than close reading', Jane Rendell, on Isobel Armstrong, in *Site Writing: The Architecture of Art Criticism* (London: I.B. Tauris, 2010), 4.

19 Healy and Weber, *There They Carved A Space,* 13.

20 de Certeau, 93.

21 Andrea Brady, 'Talking Poetics: Dialogues in Innovative Poetry', in *Mutability: Scripts for Infancy* (Chicago: University of Chicago Press, 2009), 103–34.

22 'the aesthetic ends of erasure, everyone agrees, begin with Tom Phillips', Mary Ruefle, 'On Erasure', https://www.ohio.edu/cas/quarter-after-eight/table-contents.

23 Ibid.

24 Ruefle, *A Little White Shadow* (Seattle: Wave Books, 2006), iii.

25 Ruefle, 'On Erasure.'

26 Antoine Compagnon, *La Seconde Main, ou Le travail de la citation,* trans. Marjorie Perloff, (Paris: Seuil, 1979), 173.

27 See Marjorie Perloff, *Unoriginal Genius: Poems by Other Means in the New Century* (Chicago, University of Chicago Press, 2010).

28 Brady, *Mutability: Scripts for Infancy,* (Chicago: University of Chicago Press, 2009), 109.

29 Compagnon, *La Seconde Main,* 173.

30 Ruefle, 'On Erasure.'

31 Ruefle, 'Dew,' *The Poetry Review,* Summer 2016, 106, no.2, 40–1.

32 Ruefle, 'On Beginnings,' *Madness, Rack, and Honey* (Seattle: Wave Books, 2012), 5.

33 Joe Brainard, interviewed by Anne Waldman, *Rocky Ledge* 3 (November/

December 1979), 42, in Rona Cran, 'Men with a Pair of Scissors: Joe Brainard and John Ashbery's Eclecticism,' *Joe Brainard's Art*, ed. Yasmine Shamma (Edinburgh University Press, 2020).

34 Ruefle, 'On Erasure.'

35 Anne Carson, 'Variations on the Right to Remain Silent,' *Float* (London: Jonathan Cape, 2016).

36 William Schneider, 'Interviewing in Cross-Cultural Settings,' *The Oxford Handbook of Oral History,* ed. Donald A Ritchie, (Oxford: Oxford University Press, 2011), 56.

37 Ruefle, 'On Erasure.'

References

Agee, James. *Now Let Us Praise Famous Men.* London: Peter Owen, 1965.

Armstrong, Isobel. 'Textual harassment: The ideology of close reading, or how close is close?' *Textual Practice,* June 2008, 401–20. https://doi.org/10.1080/09502369508582228

Auerbach, Jake. dir. *20 Sites, n Years.* 2016.

Bergvall, Caroline, *Drift.* Callicoon: Nightboat Books, 2014.

Bergvall, Caroline. 'Pressure Points.' *How2 Journal,* 2007. www.asu.edu/piper/how2journal/vol_3_no_3/bergvall/pdfs/bergvall-pressure-points.pdf

Brady, Andrea. *Mutability: Scripts for Infancy.* Chicago: University of Chicago Press, 2009.

de Certeau, Michel. *The Practice of Everyday Life.* Translated by Steven Rendall. London: University of California Press: 1988.

de Certeau, Michel. *The Practice of Everyday Life, Volume 2: Living & Cooking.* Translated by Timothy J. Tomasik. Minneapolis: University of Minnesota Press, 1998.

Carson, Anne. 'Variations on the Right to Remain Silent.' *Float.* London: Jonathan Cape, 2016.

Cran, Rona. 'Joy, Sobriety, Nutty Poetry.' *On Joe Brainard,* ed. Yasmine Shamma. Edinburgh: Edinburgh University Press, forthcoming, 10.

Debord, Guy. 'Théorie de la dérive.' *The Situationist International Anthology.* Translated by Ken Knabb. Minneapolis: Bureau of Public Secrets, 2006.

Healy, Claire and Emilia Weber. *There They Carved a Space.* (Script 2016).

Murren, Gwendolen 'Review of *Drift* by Caroline Bergvall.' *Chicago Review,* 59, no 1/2 (Fall 2014/Winter 2015), 276–80.

Olesen, Virginia L., and Elvi Whittaker. 'Role-making in participant observation: processes in the research-actor relationship.' *Human Organisation* 26, 1967, 273–81.

Orton, Harold, and Nathalia Wright. *A Word Geography of England.* New York: Souvenir, 1974.

Perloff, Marjorie. *Unoriginal Genius: Poems By Other Means in the New Century.* Chicago: University of Chicago Press, 2010.

Rendell, Jane. *Site Writing: The Architecture of Art Criticism.* London: I.B. Tauris, 2010.

Ritchie, Donald A., ed. *The Oxford Handbook of Oral History.* Oxford: Oxford University Press, 2011.

Ruefle, Mary, *A Little White Shadow.* Seattle: Wave Books, 2006.

Ruefle, Mary. 'Dew.' *The Poetry Review,* 106, no. 2 (summer 2016): 40–1.

Ruefle, Mary. *Madness, Rack, and Honey.* Seattle: Wave Books, 2012.

Ruefle, Mary. 'On Erasure.' https://www.ohio.edu/cas/quarter-after-eight/table-con-tents.

Thurston, Scott. *Talking Poetics: Dialogues in Innovative Poetry.* London: Shearsman Books, 2011.

Whittaker, Elvi. 'The ethnography of James Agee: the moral and existential accounta-bility of knowledge.' *Canadian Review of Sociology,* 15 (1978): 425–32.

Transit of the Megaliths: The Back End

Nicholas Brooks

In thinking through the inception of this film the visitation of certain places or references suddenly seems not so important as the notion of departure. I knew that I wanted to take something away, the way you might take a relation away on a trip and usher all of the contingencies that person, place and opportunity incur.

Nicholas Brooks, *Transit of the Megaliths* (UK, 2013). Objects modelled on those from Paul Nash's painting *Equivalents for the Megaliths* come to rest on a car roof.

The passengers were to be some odd personages. A disparate collection of shapes and motifs, spare parts and associated items, associated with a journey, a departure in itself: roof rack, ratchet straps, plywood.

Associated with a painting – things in a field having no right to be there – but auguring a new right of positioning, a new dispensation of displacement. Passing through although not moving. Having temporary, timeless leave to remain. Out of time: cycling through a portentous instant. Quite solid.

Paul Nash, *Equivalents for the Megaliths*, 1935, oil on canvas.

An image of a flatbed truck meets the strange, very public interiority of Paul Nash's *Equivalents for the Megaliths*. Large barrels which know what they're for. Panels for an unknowable construction. Segments of a geometry as yet incomplete, replete in an awkward posse, parked in some dull spot.

The flatbed truck has that same portable theatre of the wrong, the unmade, the defiantly solid. Growing wrongness in every new scene, with every new juxtaposition of torus and ditch, cylinder and car park, air filter and ploughed field. My film *Transit of the Megaliths* was commissioned for display in a multi-storey car park overlooking London, and vehicles were on my mind.

Here also begins the notion of the *back end:* that which

Nicholas Brooks, *Transit of the Megaliths*, (UK, 2013). The idealised solids of Nash's images are replaced by more utilitarian objects.

lingers and proliferates behind the interface, behind the stage, behind a visible service or an operation. The back end is plain to see but can't be glued together in the senses. The components don't have recognisable causal relations. The noses aren't on their faces. In an economy of visual contiguity the back end suffers collapse into its discrete parts, heterogeneous and a problem.

In Nash's *Equivalents for the Megaliths* back-end objects have accumulated into mid-field, mid-frame to stand in for another composition, in lieu of another cast that was acceptable prior to this. Other subjects have become inflated and unfit, and suddenly these disparates fit; they are the only workable motifs left. They have drifted in from the sides of the road to stand in, and their silhouettes embed indelibly through time, bleeding through reproductions and imitations into the blueprints of landmarks and device housings. Contemporary resuscitations of their un-deadness, pressed into service for the service industry.

Their wrongness circulates, sleeping in its purposefulness, with their zombie genealogy being part of their signification. Positioned in a car park, the film I made pitched Nash's *Night Bombardment* against Southwark's Shard. Partners in

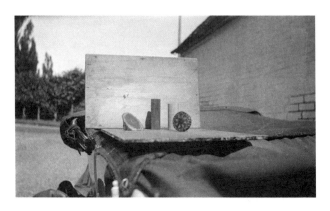

Paul Nash, *Black and White Negative, Still Life on Car Roof*, 1934.

triangularity-against-a-flat-background. Sleeping signs of relatedness to function, of powerful direction visually and of incongruity with their surroundings.

In the film, the shard / triangle flits about, stops over, undergoing a circular odyssey. Its journey, as could be with any tour, becomes the locus of its articulation. Articulating itself near this, passing this, leaving this. Heading around. The play was an intentional indulgence, as with the replacement by Nash of

Nicholas Brooks, *Transit of the Megaliths*, (UK, 2013).
The shard / triangle parks in a lime pit.

       Transit of the Megaliths

Avebury's megaliths, with his new actors that would do to fill in with unguessed purpose the enigma of their predecessors. Whatever you chose would be an indulgence and a placeholder: following the logic of the somnambulations of forms across media, these objects could depart from one diorama to the next, no problem. Use and misuse become equivalent in this world: back-of-the-lorry philosophy put to work.

Nicholas Brooks, *Transit of the Megaliths*, (UK, 2013).

As a work practicing migration, the film necessarily takes it up as part of its subject. But with the interest in Nash and his visual inception of a particular moment in the movement and purpose of forms – forms dug perhaps from the quarry of European modernism, found in a field in Sussex – another migration is alluded to. A migration which, following the growth and expansion of the industrial wealth of Europe and its global tradepartners, entails that the sublime of the manufactured, and the back-end of that manufacture enter visual life. Entering and ending up in fields which for Nash were not yet earmarked green belts.

Remembering Paul Virilio's dromoscopy – the sort of dashboard-isation of experience brought about by the combined hex of car and road, this flow of the manufactured into our direct gaze seems to lead ultimately to a displacement of all landscape as such, or rather the re-rendering of scenery as subordinate to the technology of its consumption. This suddenly appears to be written large across the whole rural topography: its descent into becoming a back-end conduit to the foreground/interface of the city, its façades and the curses roads multiply upon roads.

Nicholas Brooks, *Transit of the Megaliths* (UK, 2013). Installation view of the film projected in a tunnel made from lorry tarpaulin.

In *The Machine Stops*, a prescient 1909 sci-fi short story, E. M. Forster watches his characters traverse, in windowless airships, the terrain between the subterranean-interface-dominated cells they inhabit. It's no longer necessary to look out of the window as 'the landscape' has become culturally redundant. It is this sort of redundancy that already can be seen as an inkling in Nash's paintings. He is devoted to a series of landscapes in which changing enigmas are generators of colour and form, but there is also a restriction and caution there, a curtailment.

A pre-sentiment that they persist despite deranging forces. There in his work are invaded landscapes put upon by foreign forms, and in some cases completely constituted by them.

In the film the 'landscape' is very much in evidence, though somehow infected by the cylinders and rectilinear elements that are strapped to the car's roof rack. The tree's silhouettes conform to sharp, arbitrary diagonal lines, and improbable tubular apartment blocks or conference centres emerge from beyond the horizon. This is to recognise a slow convergence of geometric domination via 'figure,' and geometric domination via 'ground,' the two fundaments of the picture plane. This encroachment begun with mechanised agriculture, road building, and met eventually from the other side with the prefabricated metal panel of the out-of-town retail shed – enacts in this game of genealogy a slow corralling of the senses; the replacement of body parts with synthetic elements may go unnoticed until suddenly everything develops a metallic taste.

In my transit of the megaliths there is still 'landscape,' and the forms might seem to circulate happily. Adaptation and

Paul Nash, *Totes Meer* (Dead Sea), 1940–41, oil on canvas.

curiosity thrive amongst the living and the undead in the world of the film. It is by way of recognising our habilitation of the enigmas of these form-zombies surrounding us that the film determines to enjoy their company on this excursion. In deference to the pleasure of wrongness and the friendly way we adopt wayward forms and dangle them into our lives, there appears the lost ornament and the boot-sale salvage among all the others. The pleasure of holidaying amongst the ruins is shared, after all, by both people and objects.

Nicholas Brooks, *Transit of the Megaliths* (UK, 2013).

Transit of the Megaliths

Ektoras Arkomanis is a filmmaker and a lecturer in architectural history and theory at the School of Art, Architecture and Design, London Metropolitan University. His research revolves around urban areas which remain at the margins of history, planning and the city's conscience. He uses film for its capacity to preserve and explore, but is ultimately interested in what it omits and its inadequacy in describing things that are no longer there. He is currently editing his second feature film, *A Season in the Olive Grove*, a documentary about the area of Eleonas in Athens.

Lana Askari holds a PhD in Social Anthropology with Visual Media from the University of Manchester. She studied political science and anthropology at University College Utrecht and Cambridge University, and was trained in documentary filmmaking at the Granada Centre for Visual Anthropology at Manchester. Her films have been screened at various festivals, such as the RAI film festival, Freiburger Film Forum and the Kurdish Film Days Amsterdam. She is interested in the anthropology of the Middle East, particularly in Kurdistan, and issues of migration, youth, time and urban planning. Her doctoral research, for which she produced the films *Bridge to Kobane* (2016) and *Future Factory* (2018), focused on how people in Iraqi Kurdistan imagine and plan their future in times of crisis. She currently works at a Dutch consultancy company which focuses on achieving social impact through the public sector.

Edwina Attlee is a lecturer in history and theory of architecture at the School of Art, Architecture and Design, London Metropolitan University, and a Teaching Fellow at the Bartlett School of Architecture, University College London. She is the author of two pamphlets of poetry, *Roasting Baby* (if a leaf falls press) and *the cream* (clinic). She has co-edited *Gross Ideas: Tales of Tomorrow's Architecture* (London: Architecture Foundation, 2019).

Maeve Brennan is an artist based in London, working with moving image and installation. Her practice explores the political and historical resonance of material and place. Recent solo exhibitions include *Listening in the Dark*, Wäinö Aaltonen Museum of Art, Finland (2019); *The Goods*, KUB Billboards at Kunsthaus Bregenz, Austria (2018); *The Drift*, Chisenhale Gallery, London; *The Drift*, Spike Island, Bristol; *The Drift*, The Whitworth, University of Manchester (all 2017); and *Jerusalem Pink*, OUTPOST, Norwich (2016). Her films have been screened internationally at festivals including FILMADRID, Sheffield Doc Fest, and International Film Festival Rotterdam, where she was shortlisted for the Tiger Shorts Award 2018. Brennan was educated at Goldsmiths, University of London and was a fellow of the Home Workspace Program at Ashkal Alwan in Beirut (2013–14). She was awarded the Jerwood/FVU Award 2018 and is the Stanley Picker Fine Art Fellow 2019.

Nicholas Brooks is a London-based artist working with film, sculpture and installation. His work ranges across subjects such as archaeology, early technologies and future dystopias. He graduated with his MFA from the Slade in 2011, and has since had shows at MOT international, Vitrine, Jerwood Space, Project/Number and the Turner Contemporary, among others. His films have been shown internationally at venues such as the Garage Museum of Contemporary Art in Moscow, the Rotterdam and Berlinale film festivals, Reina Sofia Madrid, and have toured venues across the UK, the United States and Japan. He has lectured at the Cass School of Art, Architecture and Design (London Metropolitan University), the Architectural Association and Central Saint Martins (University of the Arts).

Sirah Foighel Brutmann and Eitan Efrat are members of the artist-run collective Messidor. They are Brussels-based artists working in the audio-visual field and teaching at Erg, Brussels. Their practice focuses on the performative aspects of the moving image. They are interested in the spatial and durational potentialities in the reading of still and moving images, the relations between spectatorship and history, the temporality of narratives and memory, and the material surfaces of image production. Their works have been shown in duo exhibitions in Kunsthalle Basel (CH), Argos (BE) and CAC Delme (FR); at group exhibitions in Argos, Brussels (BE); Museum für Kunst und Gewerbe, Hamburg (DE);

Portikus, Frankfurt (DE); Museumcultuur Strombeek (BE); Skulpturenmuseum Glaskasten Marl (DE) Jeu de Paume, Paris (FR) and STUK, Leuven (BE) and in film festivals such as EMAF, Osnabrück (DE); Atonal, Berlin (DE); Doclisboa (PT); Underdox Munich (DE); Oberhausen Film Festival, (DE); Les Rencontres International, Paris and Berlin; IDFA, Amsterdam (NL); New Horizons, Wroclaw (PL); Oberhausen Film Festival, (DE); Kasseler Dokfest, Kassel, (DE); Rotterdam Film Festival, (NL); Media City, Windsor, (CA); Images, Toronto (CA); Planstik, Dublin (IE); November Film Festival, London (UK); Visite, Antwerp (BE); Bratislava Film Festival (SK); 25FPS Zagreb (HR).

Sander Hölsgens is a writer and filmmaker, and the co-founder of Pushing Borders and Field Recordings. He obtained his PhD from the Bartlett School of Architecture, University College London, for which he researched skateboarding in South Korea. He currently works at Rijksuniversiteit Groningen as a post-doctoral researcher in the NWO-funded project Exploring Journalism's Limits.

Sasha Litvintseva is an artist-filmmaker and writer-researcher whose work is situated on the uncertain thresholds of human/nonhuman, inside/outside and perceptible/communicable, the intersection of media and the ecology and history of science. She is deeply invested in moving image as an embodied, affective medium. Her work has been exhibited worldwide, including Berlinale; Rotterdam International

Film Festival; Videobrasil; The Moscow Biennale for Young Art; Wroclaw Media Art Biennale; Sonic Acts; Mumok, Vienna, including solo presentations at Institute of Contemporary Art, London; Berlinische Galerie, Modern Art Museum Berlin; Museum of Contemporary Art, Chicago; Courtisane Film Festival; Union Docs, New York, among others. She is a lecturer in Film Theory and Practice at Queen Mary University of London, and is currently completing a PhD at Goldsmiths University, which proposes the concept of geological filmmaking. Her academic writing has appeared in special issues of *Environmental Humanities* and *Transformations* journals, and in publications by Sonic Acts.

Maha Maamoun is a Cairo-based artist. Her work examines the form, function and currency of common cultural visual and literary images as an entry point to investigating the cultural fabric that we weave and are woven into. She also works collaboratively on independent publishing and curatorial projects. She is a founding member of the Contemporary Image Collective (CiC), an independent non-profit space for art and culture founded in Cairo in 2004, and a co-founder of the independent publishing platform Kayfa ta. Her work has been shown in exhibitions and biennials including: Constructing the world: Art and economy 1919–39 and 2008–18, Kunsthalle Mannheim (2018); Strange Days: Memories of the Future – Store X and New Museum (2018); The Time is Out of Joint – Sharjah Art Foundation (2016); Century of Centuries – SALT (2015); Like Milking a Stone – Rosa Santos Gallery (2015); The Night of Counting the Years – Fridericianum (2014); Here and Elsewhere – New Museum; Ten Thousand Wiles and a Hundred Thousand Tricks – Meeting Points 7; Forum Expanded – Berlinale 64; Transmediale; Objects in Mirror are Closer than they Appear, Tate Modern; 9th Gwangju Biennale; Momentarily Learning from Mega Events, Makan, Amman; Second World: Where is Progress Progressing, Steirischer Herbst; The End of Money, Witte de With; Sharjah Biennial 10; Mapping Subjectivity, MoMA; Live Cinema, Philadelphia Museum of Art; Ground Floor America, Den Frie Centre of Contemporary Art; The Future of Tradition / The Tradition of Future, Haus der Kunst.

Katrin Wahdat is an architect based in London. She wrote the present essay as a postgraduate student of architecture at the School of Art, Architecture and Design, London Metropolitan University, under the supervision of Edwina Attlee.

Acknowledgements

The editor would like to thank all the contributing artists and writers for their poetic reflections on films and places; the publisher, Cours de Poétique, and in particular Joseph Kohlmaier for his sensitivity to the material and for an ideal working relationship; all students, past and present, of the course Cinema and the City, which for a decade-and-a-half has been a special place for re-viewing films. The course was the inspiration for the book, which grew out of a series of open lectures at the School of Art, Architecture and Design in 2017, and was made possible with a research grant by London Metropolitan University. Thanks for their support to Andrew Stone, Dean of the school, and Anne Markey, Head of Research Policy and Implementation at London Metropolitan University. Special thanks to Gosia Ostrowska for her support and encouragement throughout.

Credits

Cover image
Maeve Brennan, *Jerusalem Pink* (2016)

All images by the authors except: p. 63, by Serafeim Arkomanis; p. 132, courtesy of Tom Phillips; p. 141, by Harold Orton and Natalia Wright; pp. 153, 155 (top), 158 © Tate Enterprises.

Published by Cours de Poétique, London, in 2020
Copyright © Cours de Poétique 2020
Copyright © The authors 2020

The book was designed, typeset and made into pages by Lisa Stephanides and Joseph Kohlmaier at Polimekanos / Cours de Poétique in London. The cover was designed by Joseph Kohlmaier. Proofs of the pages in progress were read by Janine Su. The book was printed and bound by Graphius in Belgium.

ISBN 978-0-9935317-2-9
www.coursdepoetique.org

Each copy of *Migrations* comes with an access code to view the authors' films on Cours de Poétique's website.

To view the films, please register your copy on coursdepoetique.org/migrations/media